PUKI HORPOCKET PRESENTS

ROY

THE MOST CHAOTIC MIDLIFE
CRISIS IN COSMIC HISTORY

EARTH EDITION BY
ZACHRY WHEELER

eBook ISBN: 978-1-954153-02-8
Paperback ISBN: 978-1-954153-01-1
Hardcover ISBN: 978-1-954153-11-0
Edited by Jennifer Amon
Published by Mayhematic Press

B.R.A.G. Medallion Honoree
Readers' Favorite 5-Star Selection

For mom, dad, and bro,
who always encouraged me to
explore this bonkers universe.

EARTH EDITION

Greetings, Earthling!

My name is Zachry Wheeler and I'm a science fiction novelist based on Earth. I was chosen to serve as translator for all terrestrial editions of *Puki Horpocket Presents*, a literary series beloved throughout the universe.

It's been a great honor.

It's also been super stressful.

Decoding an alien tongue is daunting at a baseline, let alone through the prestigious lens of Puki Horpocket. He is renowned for his unique blend of commentary, interviews, and dramatic depictions. My job is to stick the landing for human readers. I sincerely hope that I do his words justice, but admittedly, I sometimes feel like a toddler translating Orwell.

The Durangoni Space Station is home to countless species and cultures, and thus, countless lexicons. Some things are universal, like beer. Other things are regional, like atmo barriers on artificial oceans. Some things are truly horrifying and do not warrant translation, regardless of their pop culture equivalents.

I did my best, but aliens be weird, y'all.

Puki Horpocket tales are chock-full of excitement, debauchery, and blatant disregard for delicate sensibilities. Fair warning: the language is lewd and the characters are crude, so keep your wits inside the vehicle and enjoy the ride.

CHAPTER 1

It is a well-known fact that every being in the universe is biologically compelled to talk smack. If three beings exist on a planet, it is inevitable that two of them will gossip about the third. In addition, most beings are convinced that their tiny corner of the cosmos is much more important than it actually is. But every so often, one of those beings will rise from the muck to stamp their mark on history.

This is the tale of one such being.

But before we begin, I must introduce myself. My name is Puki Horpocket. I am an editor at large for the Definitive Directory of Durangoni, the panoptic mega-wiki for life aboard the largest space station in the universe. Durangoni is a planet-sized colossus. It houses a trillion active residents, all of whom access the directory for their daily needs. And to ensure those needs are met, the station employs a massive staff of writers, reporters, editors, and baristas, all wholly dedicated to keeping the directory au courant.

Tenants consult the directory for a variety of reasons. Perhaps they need a ship mechanic, or a warm meal at a mid-level restaurant. Perhaps they would like to fist a dominurb while wearing a tutu inside a womp-brothel. The directory is an indiscriminate depot that treats all inquiries alike. No tracking, no history, no snarky comments or unearned ratings, just a freely accessible index of current and relevant data. Under a veil of complete anonymity, anyone in the midst of a titanic midlife crisis can easily search for a hot enema of sinful delight.

Enter Roy.

As strange as it may sound, nobody knows his last name. I devoted countless hours to this mystery, all of which uncovered bupkis. Not a single employer knew his full name, nor is Roy short for anything more distinguished. In fact, he is listed as "Roy" in the civilian archives. Astoundingly, in the grand totality of station operation, not a single Roy resident thought to register as just Roy.

That is, until Roy.

He is, for all intents and purposes, just Roy.

I never met Roy, but I came to know him through his friends, enemies, and confidants. I interviewed several along the way, many of whom are featured in this very book. Most will be new to your eyes, but some carry infamous reputations that you will undoubtedly recognize. After all, one does not attain a legendary status without crossing some of the universe's most notorious inhabitants.

Roy's tale was thrust upon me during a jaunt to the outer rings. I was working on a field piece about district taverns, which involved a dreadful amount of sensory-hostile interviews. However, what began as a vapid chore would blossom into a full-blown obsession. It became abundantly clear that every gutter rat, every bar slag, and every spittoon-filling whoremonger upheld Roy as some sort of folk hero.

I wanted to know more, so I went digging.

What I found was a treasure trove of lunacy.

The story of Roy is so burdened by stupidity, so marred by absurdity, that it bewitched me from the start. It is a tale wrought with love, loss, danger, and a healthy dose of folly. In other words, it ticks all the right boxes for a whimsical train wreck.

I must preface anything further with an important disclaimer. To tell the story of Roy is to tell the story of "The Incident."

Every citizen of Durangoni knows about The Incident, but few are aware that Roy was the instigator. To be fair, the term "instigator" may be a tad generous. Roy was many things, but a cunning mastermind he was not. I am forced to use "was" in reference to Roy because no one has seen or heard from him since. The Incident is capitalized because it managed to affect the entire population, thus earning its definite article and prominent lettering. But to be honest, the event was so jarring and disruptive that I firmly believe it should be referenced in all caps.

Yes, even as an editor.

So without further ado, let us begin to unravel this tale of intrigue. As with any good story, it starts with a kerfuffle.

*　*　*

The charred impacts of plasma bolts stained the interior of a popular brewpub. A firefight had erupted a few days earlier, an exceedingly rare occurrence inside Durangoni. The station was a neutral harbor to an extreme degree, even housing a private security force that rivaled the best militaries in the quadrant. Firearms of any kind were strictly forbidden. A zero-tolerance policy included flash flogging for violators, so residents moseyed through the corridors without much regard for safety. Therefore, staring at the blackened remains of plasma fire conjured the same confusion as an abstract painting.

Toppled chairs and tables cluttered the interior, the remnants of patrons making their hasty exits. Broken glass and shattered plates littered the floor, creating a labyrinth of foot-stabbing fun. The stench of rotting food floated around the pub like a wandering fart that refused to dissipate. The dark wood and rustic metal hid some of the filth, but the exploded terrace was difficult to ignore. Security had completed its investigation, leaving a swarm of maintenance crews to tend to repairs. The constant roar of saws, drills, and laser cutters infected the space with a rumble of restoration.

The commotion created quite the nuisance for anyone within earshot. The terrace overlooked an open-air garden that spanned several stories. Balconies surrounded the space, which served as a hub for numerous galleries and restaurants. A prime location for any proprietor, should they afford the rent. The pub was an old establishment and one of the first to claim the area. As such, it enjoyed lower rent and grandfathered perks. It rested along the third tier and protruded like an unsightly pimple, given its ritzy neighbors. This rang especially true as spectators gazed upon the splintered shards that used to be its terrace.

Its neighbor across the way was impacted the most, in a very literal sense. On top of having a front-row seat to the battle, it had endured a barrage of wayward blasts. It also emitted the growls of restoration, complete with yellow tape to underscore the inconvenience.

A handful of flowering vines dangled from an overhead lattice. Before the assault, a thick assortment of foliage had hung inside the hollow as a waterfall of greenery, the handiwork of a famous artist. The plasma fire had ripped through the display like a flock of machetes, dropping most of it to the floor. A mess of leaves and vines clogged the sidewalks and fountains, creating an aggravating cleanup for plumbers and gardeners.

One such plumber stood ankle-deep inside a small fountain while staring at the shattered terrace. A pair of soiled overalls hung from his meager shoulders and tucked into a set of knee-high waders. He was an average creature with an average height and an average build. His hybrid-like body resembled a salamander that decided to become human, but lost interest halfway through. He carried some extra belly weight, not that he minded, as impressing the opposite sex had been abandoned long ago. His balding head and blotchy green skin amplified a midlife persona. To say this chap was forgettable would be to undermine the very notion of memory.

He sighed and dropped his gaze to the fountain water, once clean and crystal clear, but now dark with soot and debris. The filtering unit beneath the surface belched and gurgled as it tried and failed to sift through the sludge. Roy cringed and turned for his toolbox, only to meet the bulging eyes of a sentient man-pear.

"Shit fuck!" Roy said and sloshed backwards.

Duncan laughed, causing his plump belly to poke out from beneath a plaid work shirt. Thick gray skin, stumpy limbs, and a bulbous torso created the portrait of a land-tromping manatee. His species enjoyed a lush homeworld with low gravity, so life aboard the station was challenging at a baseline. He never complained, though. Duncan rolled with the punches better than anyone. A pair of work slacks started to slide off his waist, cueing a well-practiced grip-n-tug. His laughter slowed to a hearty exhale. "Heya, Roy," he said with a core-cocked accent (the local equivalent of a Midwestern car salesman).

"You really need to wear a bell, man."

"And give up my ninja-like stealthitude?"

Roy rolled his eyes. "Dunc, you're a ninja like a ... um, like ..."

Duncan nodded and motioned to continue.

"Dammit," Roy said, adding a heavy sigh.

"Wow. Not like you to miss a good rib poke."

Roy frowned and glanced at the terrace. "Just not feeling like myself today."

"You depressed again?"

"I'm always depressed, you know that."

"No, I mean, like, uber depressed. Long weekend at the Kink Rinks depressed."

Roy raised an eyebrow. "There's an idea."

"You can always return to group."

Roy huffed. "No thanks. If I wanted to listen to someone drone on about their feelings, I'd phone your mother."

Duncan chuckled, then leaned forward to rummage through Roy's toolbox. He grunted and wheezed on the way down, like a sumo wrestler trying to touch his toes. Dropping to a knee, he paused for a breather before reaching inside and withdrawing a pair of scissors. The struggle back to his feet was equally cumbersome. He tested the scissors for their scissoring scissorness, then nodded with approval. "Yes, these will do nicely."

Roy had studied the effort with little emotion, content to watch his friend struggle through the simple tasks of living. If anything, it made him feel better about his own miseries. "You're a fucking gardener, Duncan."

"True fact," he said with a wide smile.

"How is it possible that you didn't bring any shears?"

"Oh I did, but they're way over there." Duncan pointed to his satchel, which rested on the sidewalk a few meters away.

"Get back to work, assholes," the foreman said as he strolled by.

Roy and Duncan turned to the hairy beast.

"Piss off, Clancy," Roy said as a canned retort.

The beast stopped in its tracks and whipped an angered gaze to Roy, revealing knobby tusks, puffy lips, and lemon-yellow eyes. An orange vest hung from its sturdy shoulders, which fanned through the air when he spun towards the insubordinate plumber. The beast stepped forward and loomed over the fountain like a lion claiming a waterhole. His eyes narrowed as bull-like nostrils expelled puffs of heated breath. "What did you say to me?"

Roy maintained his apathetic stare. "Sorry, I misspoke. What I meant to say was, lick my salty nether sack."

Duncan snorted.

The beast's eyes widened. "You insolent little shit nugget."

"Like the ones on your hairy asshole?"

"I can fire you right now."

"But you won't."

The fountain gurgled and spat a dollop of mud onto Roy's leg.

Clancy glanced at Duncan, who smiled back through his always-cheerful demeanor. The beast sighed, mumbled some curses, then softened his tone. "We still on for The Pipes tonight?"

"That's the plan," Duncan said.

"Assuming we can clean this up in time," Roy said as he glanced around the filth.

"Ain't no way," Clancy said. "We have a bunch of new regulations to satisfy, so plan on being here all week. On the upside, the budget has ballooned with the schedule. You got a full green light on overtime, so milk it all you like."

"Nice," Duncan said.

Roy groaned, as per usual.

Clancy huffed and shook his head. "Jeez, Roy. Would it kill you to fake some gratitude? I could hand you a sack of money and you'd bitch about having to carry it."

Roy grimaced. "Says the salaried employee who makes more than the two of us combined."

"You say that like I didn't earn it."

"You didn't. Sandra just wanted some eye-candy in the main office."

"It's not like that at all."

"It's a little like that," Duncan said, adding a finger pinch.

"Pretty boy gets the cookie," Roy said with a hint of disdain.

Clancy sighed and glanced away.

"So what happened up there?" Duncan said, eyeing the splintered terrace.

"Yeah," Roy said. "They haven't told us shit. All we got is hearsay and rumors."

Clancy shrugged. "You know as much as I do. Some mystery goon snuck in with a plasma pistol and shot up the place. They've been pretty tight-lipped about the encounter. Oh, I did learn that some Mulgawat ladies were involved."

Roy dropped his jaw. "Are you fucking kidding me?"

"What?" Duncan said.

"My one chance to meet a Mulgawat and I missed it."

Clancy snort-chuckled. "Like you would ever be in this area for any reason. Hell, the fountain you're standing in probably costs more than you'll ever make."

Roy narrowed his eyes.

"I never knew you had a thing for Mulgawats," Duncan said.

"Not a *thing* per se. They're just so ..." Roy stammered a bit, then grinned like a creepy uncle. "Exotic."

"Oookay," Clancy said, raising his mitts. "The last thing I need is another one of your Kink Rinks recaps. Save it for The Pipes."

"You're getting the first round, salary boy."

"If I say yes, will you shut up and get back to work?"

The fountain belched a ribbon of muck onto Roy's cheek. "My

7

work fulfills me," he said without flinching.

Clancy snickered, then resumed his trek down the sidewalk. "See you guys at eight."

Duncan hook-yanked his pants and turned to Roy. "Why do you always have to be such a sourpuss?"

Roy glowered at Duncan as a wad of mud fell from his chin and plunked into the fountain.

"Ner'mind," Duncan said. "Just get through the day as best you can and we'll toss back a few frosties later."

"As if you needed to tell me."

Duncan huffed. "Tim almighty, this pity party got an end?"

Roy cracked a smile. "Fine, I yield to the court. Now piss off and trim something."

Duncan nodded and returned the smile. He tested the scissors on some imaginary vines, then waddled towards a mess of foliage.

Roy glanced down at the gurgling muck, then over to his sad little toolbox, then up to the exploded terrace. His feigned grin inverted itself as he battled a wave of dejection. He couldn't help but imagine the ruckus, the destruction, the excitement, and most importantly, the fact that he wasn't there and never would have been. Roy had slogged through the swamp of mediocrity, bound by doubt and slave to resentment. But as he stared up at the wreckage, a strange new itch infected his psyche. An itch that he had no idea how to scratch.

* * *

That was the moment.

I have watched the story of Roy from its curious start to chaotic finale. I have studied his every action, from the tiniest intonations to the galloping insanity. But that moment, that brief and beautiful moment etched into the security footage of history, ignited the flames of destiny that would entangle a trillion souls. It gives me chills to this day, watching the avatar of apathy stare into the great unknown without qualm or trepidation. That was the moment when Roy the plumber became Roy the would-be legend.

CHAPTER 2

I reviewed The Pipes for the Definitive Directory of Durangoni, which remains one of my shortest entries to date. In its entirety: "The establishment seems to exist solely to exacerbate a throbbing headache. Avoid at all costs."

In retrospect, the review may have been a tad harsh. However, this is not to say that it was in any way inaccurate, because it wasn't. The Pipes is a cauldron of noise, an audible assault from every direction. But as I delved into the story of Roy, I discovered a strange new affinity for the hideous little pub.

The Pipes is a junction room about the size of a large garage. The place gets its name from the countless pipes and conduits that cover the walls and ceiling. It's a hellish maze of metal that includes water lines, atmo ducts, everything a healthy station needs. Most junctions are properly zoned and automated, but this one had suffered from a critical design flaw. The resulting morass was so convoluted that it required a constant stream of upkeep.

Fixing the mess was deemed too disruptive, so a dedicated technician was assigned to the junction. Two weeks later, he quit. Another technician was assigned and quit the following day. A droid was assigned, but the chaotic nature of the room quickly drove it insane.

The junction became notorious for its endless cycle of hire-quit-repeat. In fact, only one technician managed to stay for longer than a month, and she was legally deaf.

But as with most bizarre conundrums, the eventual solution was equally bizarre.

Fiona was a talented mechanic who lived near the junction. One day, she met some friends at a nearby pub and proceeded to drink herself silly. As she stumbled home, she decided to swing by the junction room to see what all the fuss was about. She ducked inside and marveled at the clattering labyrinth before passing out. When she awoke, she came to a sobering realization. To quote her business proposal, "It's not that bad when you're drunk."

Her solution was simple: convert the room into a workman's pub and offer free drinks in exchange for maintenance. The station agreed and The Pipes was born. It quickly became a haven for working stiffs with limited booze budgets. Whenever a gauge popped or a fitting leaked, the most sober and qualified guest would make the repair. The strategy proved wildly successful, transforming the space from a hole of despair into a model of efficiency. (It's still a hole of despair, just a very efficient one.)

Fiona has worked there as the owner-manager since day one and also serves as a frequent bartender. The Pipes celebrated its 30th anniversary as I was compiling this book. Fiona has amassed a large and dedicated customer base, solidifying her status as a barfly matriarch. Her patrons are fiercely loyal, granting her a cult-like following. Roy was a proud member of that sect, and Fiona knew him better than most.

I remember meeting Fiona on my first visit to The Pipes. She greeted me kindly as I was stuffing wads of tissue into my ears. Her stout frame is an impressive ratio of width and height. Not overweight so much as overly brawn, complete with a pair of sumptuous bosoms that could double as deadly weapons. She embodies the role of a gruff marm, one who can toss you over a table and then soothe your ego with a mug of hot chocolate. As one of the few Earthling females living in the station, she is largely hairless, apart from a thick mane of curly locks.

Fiona was kind enough to agree to an interview for this book (and grant my request that it take place outside of the brain-battering pub). We met at a small cafe near her home, one of the countless caffeine stops inside the station. I spoke with her about Roy and his relationship with The Pipes. The following is an excerpt of that conversation.

* * *

First and foremost, I would like to thank you for agreeing to speak with me, and at the same time, apologize for my brazen review of The Pipes.

Oh sweetie, you don't need to apologize for nothin'. In fact, your review boosted my bottom line, so I should be the one to thank you.

Really? That's surprising to hear. How so?

It shouldn't be surprising at all. Your words are only heeded by a certain class of citizen. When you say "avoid at all costs," my clientele hears "a distinct lack of proper folk." That's a five-star rating for my establishment.

Be that as it may, even the uncultured have ears. How does anyone stand it inside that head-splitting horror pit?

(laughs) You get used to it. But even so, the sub-core folk have a built-in tolerance for racket, and they make up most of my patronage.

Ah, yes. Most of my readers will be unfamiliar with the sub-core, the shanty-like area that surrounds the cylindrical hub of the station. Can you give us a sympathetic insight into the citizens that call the area home?

Happy to. And thank you for asking, because these folks deserve more than a passing glance.

(I smile, nod, and swallow the not-so-veiled dig on my charac-

ter.)

As you know, Durangoni is a giant disc system, like a stack of barbell plates with the biggest in the center and the smallest at the poles. Hundreds of these discs rotate around the core, a giant cylinder that acts like a spindle.

That's actually a very effective visual. Mind if I steal it?

Please do. Anything to curb the zarpobblement (a word unique to the station, denoting a potent mixture of shock, awe, vertigo, and a sudden desire to contemplate the meaning of life).

Thank you. Apologies for the interruption, please continue.

So in order to answer your question, we must first understand how wealth is distributed inside Durangoni. As with most stations, money is traced from top to bottom. The posh live near the surface and the dregs inhabit the core, kinda like a cruise ship on a planetary scale.

Well, Durangoni is a bit different in that the core is the most expensive place to live. The sheer scale of the station requires a genius-level of engineering to keep it afloat, and the nerds that do so are held in the highest celebrity status.

But, being nerds, they ain't the type to bask on surface beaches. They just stay locked inside the core like neckbeards in a basement. As a result, the wealthy come to them. They purchase plots around the labs and build luxury abodes. For the super rich, proximity to the super nerds is seen as a status symbol. It's kinda like squatting in Bill Gates's pool house.

Bill who?

Oh, sorry. He was King of the Nerds back home, the Earth equivalent of Loomba Varvar. (King of the Nerds on Durangoni, if that wasn't obvious.)

Ah.

So tell me, what typically surrounds the wealthiest parts of a city?

The poorest ghettos.

That's right. The rich insulate themselves and wall off everything adjacent, which strips the area of business potential. But, when you apply this rule to a station the size of Durangoni, you create one of the starkest inequalities in the galaxy. We're talking a matter of meters between the richest and poorest residents. Ten meters of pure titanium to be exact, the outer casing of the inner core.

Proles will typically live near the core because that's where the work is, but that's not true on this station. The work here is near the surface because everything is automated. Durangoni represents the biggest service economy in the universe. The AI handles all the important stuff, so plumbers here ain't maintaining the water supply. They're unclogging public toilets. And the great irony is, they'll make more doing that than working respected jobs on their home planets.

And Roy was one such plumber.

Yup. And like so many, he came here to support his family.

Can you tell me more about his family and backstory?

Sure. And for the record, Roy was a good man. I understand that The Incident was a colossal shitshow. But knowing him the way I do, ain't no way he did anything out of malice. He did everything with his family in mind, despite the pain of circumstance.

Can you elaborate?

Well, Roy came here as a divorcee. He needed some extra income to support his three million children. When he—

Wait. Did you say three *million*?

Yes sir. Roy's species is a cannibalistic amphibious breed that lays millions of eggs all at once. When they hatch, they start eating each other down to about two or three. Those are the keepers that you send to college and whatnot, but until that time, the parents are liable for the lot. Roy's wife had birthed about a dozen million and the brood was down to about four million when they divorced. Their legal system favors the mother, so Roy was left broke and destitute. His child support and alimony forced him to Durangoni for better-paying work.

This is all from his side of the story, by the way. I never saw a picture of his wife or learned much about his homeworld. He was very guarded about those details. But, I do know bullshit when I hear it and he gave me no reason to doubt him. He just seemed like a bro-ken-hearted critter who fell on bad times.

Did you ever press him for details about the divorce?

Lordy no, that would've been rude. But if I had to wager a guess, I would peg her as a gold-diggin' floozy. Roy was making a decent wage as a general plumber on the station, but he still lived in the worst part of the sub-core. Even if most of your credits are going home, there's a certain level of livin' you don't want to slip beneath. Roy was always stressed about his footing, which told me that his pockets were lighter than intended.

What is life like down there?

It's noisy as hell, for one thing. Lots of engines, pumps, drones, standard rumble of upkeep. But, the Durangoni sub-core is its own special hell.

Why's that?

When the uppers started to relocate, they got all butt-hurt about the constant racket. And what happens when the rich get inconven-ienced?

Shit changes.

(nods) But rarely for the betterment of others. And so, the station decided to insulate the core to appease the bucks. Unfortunately, that included a lot of venting into the sub-core. Now it's like everyone lives on the tarmac of a busy spaceport.

I had no idea it was that bad down there.

The uppers seldom do. A ghetto is a ghetto to them. But, some are measurably worse than others. Roy endured the worst of it.

So he viewed The Pipes as a peaceful retreat.

Very much so. The Pipes are sandwiched between the ghetto and merchant lines, not quite derelict but not quite proper. It's largely ignored by the locals, but serves as a refuge for the sub-core folk. Several of my regulars travel a long way to get there.

Including Roy?

Nah. Roy lived in the same disc, so his trek was reasonable. Good thing too, because he was a handy bloke to have around. I funneled a lot of work to him, assuming he wasn't blackout drunk. He was more than happy to do it because it felt like a friendly favor. The free booze was a bonus, but not the primary reason he came. He just wanted to feel appreciated.

* * *

Fiona and I chatted for several hours before parting ways. I offered to amend my review, given her kindness and fresh perspective. She refused, noting that a first impression is where honesty lives. Fiona was a fount of insight, a fruitful springboard into a frantic investigation. While the morsels were plenty, it was the last line that stuck out the most.

Roy was an underappreciated nobody.

Hardly a groundbreaking revelation, but it provided a necessary foundation. Of course Roy was capable of sparking The Incident. He was starving for gratitude.

CHAPTER 3

After a full day of cleanup, the garden floor rested under a normal layer of filth. A notable improvement, given the original mayhem. Robotic dumpsters carried off the debris while brooms and mops tended to the remainder. Most workers had called it a day, but some were content to milk the overtime.

Fountain filters were busy returning their pools to a crystal clear persuasion. An open porthole belched steam as a socket wrench echoed from the depths. Soon after, the cranking stopped and the wrench flew out of the shaft, clank-landing near its toolbox home. A greasy Roy poked his head out the port. He inhaled a lungful of garden air, then grunted with exhaustion as he climbed out of the hole.

Roy stood up straight, arched his back, and rolled his shoulders. Every joint pop and bone crackle drew a cringe and pucker. He capped it off with a few neck rolls, one of which caught a view of a hologram wall clock.

"Shit," he said with a stymied tone, like a father forgetting to pick up his son from soccer practice. Roy double-checked his comdev, just in case the wall clock was lying out of spite. He could greet his chums in time, but the trip would be hurried and his personal hygiene would be less than ideal. Not that he had much choice, so he gathered his wayward tools and stuffed them into the box without much care for order. A grimy rag served as a mobile shower. He dunked it into the fountain and wiped his face, transforming his filthy complexion into a mildly dirty one. The rag dropped to the floor as he unhooked his jacket from a nearby lamppost. A no-look grab lifted the toolbox and he was off to meet his social obligations.

The hasty exit resulted in some stumbles and curses as he weaved through the garden maze. A standard day in the world of Roy, but no less irritating. Locals gave him a wide berth when he slipped into the corridors, likely due to the one-two punch of aromas and grumbles. The stench forced many into the walls, like a school of fish avoiding a passing shark.

A short jaunt later, he arrived at the nearest pod train station. Durangoni, being a planetary behemoth, needed a massive transport system to shuttle its trillion inhabitants from port to port. The solution was a spaghetti-like network of maglev tubes that shot pods around the station like a pinball machine. Each pod was an independent vessel that held a max capacity of two dozen lifeforms, assuming average heights and weights. The pods managed their own routes, but could also form trains for added efficiency. They could even pass through the open space between each ring, using specialized ports and tracks. In addition, their gyroscopic design kept them upright in relation to the core, no matter what direction they traveled. This allowed the tube system to snake anywhere it damn well pleased.

Roy stood to one side of a crowded pod with every other passenger crammed to the opposite wall and trying not to vomit. They all stared at Roy with cringing faces while Roy maintained a lazy-eyed stare right back at them. He killed time by making awkward eye contact with the most revolted expressions.

The ping of an approaching stop cued Roy to release his grip on an overhead strap, much to the relief of everyone on board. The pod slowed to a halt and the doors slid open, releasing a puff of odor that turned some unsuspecting heads nearby. Roy moseyed out into a small station, little more than a drab gray box that connected service tunnels. In fact, one could discern the depth of any train depot based solely on the bore factor of its interior. Unpainted panels and a sad lack of decor marked the transition from merch to maint districts. Paneling disappeared entirely when pods dropped into the sub-core. Station management deemed them unnecessary, as dregs would simply rip them from the walls and sell them for scrap.

Roy strolled through the mouth of a service corridor, a large semicircle with laser-etched letters. No holograms or fancy names at that level, just cold coordinates that reminded tenants how little the uppers cared about them. Roy's toolbox clattered with every lumbering step. The crowd maintained its forward stare as a parade of tired feet clanked along the walkway. Lighting strips bathed the passage under the harsh glow of a gas station restroom. Roy switched the box to his other hand and rolled away some soreness. A burly brute shoulder-checked him from behind, causing Roy to lose his grip. The box hit the floor, popped its lid, and coughed some tools into the tunnel. The beast smirked over his shoulder and kept walking.

"The hell is your problem?" Roy said.

The beast ignored him.

"Yo! I'm talking to you, shit nugget!"

The beast stopped in its tracks, as did most of the crowd.

"That's right, the tubby fuck with the tiny cock!"

The crowd went silent.

The beast turned to Roy, revealing its scaly skin and decidedly un-tubby frame. Radically muscled, more like it, the kind of brute that lurked in the dark corners of gyms where mortals dare not tread. Everyone else pushed to the walls, forming an arena of conflict. The beast lifted its chin and stared at Roy over a wide and blocky jaw, as if the jaw itself had also hit the gym. He snorted through a pair of gaping nostrils and flexed a pair of pecs that could double as manhole covers.

The monster was two Roys tall and a full Roy wide, creating a showdown that would make most Roys crap their pants. But not this Roy. This Roy was excited, eager even, because he had two distinct advantages. One, Durangoni Security would never allow such an event to transpire, so confrontations were little more than vanity struts. Should a fight come to actual blows, stun rods along the ceiling would knock them both out. And two, Roy's species wielded a peculiar form of natural defense, one that he could summon at will. It provided no boons to strength or dexterity, but the psychological effects were devastating.

"Say that again," the beast said with a deep and graveled tone. He took a step forward, expecting Roy to recoil.

Roy did no such thing. Instead, his bulging eyes frosted over, as if suddenly possessed. A gurgling sound erupted from his throat, the result of boiling stomach acid. The vile concoction climbed his esophagus and foamed through his mouth, spilling onto the floor like a fountain of dry ice. Croaks and neck twitches created the image of a demonic gremlin. His voice completed the transformation, dropping into a raspy seethe.

"I said." Roy took a step forward. "You're a tubby fuck." Another step. "With a tiny cock." Another step.

The brute hesitated, much to the surprise of everyone watching. His eyes widened as a confused brain fought through a loop of fear and emasculation.

A tense silence fell between them.

"Um ..." the beast said, which Roy heard as *Come at me bro!*

Roy hissed and gave charge.

The beast yelped, then spun around and sprinted down the corridor.

Roy scuffed to a stop and smirked as the brute disappeared around a corner. "Yeah, that's what I thought."

The hum of a maintenance droid broke the tension as it fluttered in to mop the floor. Roy moseyed back to his toolbox, careful to step around his own gunk. He wiped his mouth with a sleeve as his eyes slowly defogged. The gathered mass watched his every move, trying to make sense of what just happened. Roy ignored them. He gathered the spilled tools and continued on his way. The crowd lost interest soon after and the arena closed. The roars of conversation filled the tunnel as foot traffic resumed its normal pace.

Roy grinned as he sauntered down the corridor. The confrontation had added a few minutes to his arrival time, but it was a worthwhile inconvenience. A public scuffle was a rare treat and he never backed down from a fight. They seldom ended with shocks and the risk was worth the stress relief, especially given Roy's uniquely revolting talent. At the very least, random tussles served as great pub fodder.

Roy emerged into an open bazaar teeming with merchants. It carried the same chaos of a crowded mall, but the hucksters there were offering tools and fittings instead of clothes and jewelry. Industrial lights hung from the ceiling, punching through clouds of dust. Roy scanned for deals as he hiked through the clutter. He made it to the other side without breaking stride and continued down the next corridor.

Several rights and a few lefts later, Roy ducked into a residential shaft. The roar of traffic quieted, leaving the whine of the sub-core. At this level, the station emitted a constant thrum, everything from air reclaimers to fuel processors. Even so, Roy much preferred the racket of machines to the racket of people. His own steps found his ears again, drawing a brief smile. He passed a numbered door every few meters, the tiny apartment homes of anyone needing to save some credits. The passage ended at a small foyer where a few alien blokes were in mid-chat. A single gray door was attached to the space, featuring *The Pipes* etched into a nondescript plaque. To the average passerby, it may as well have been a janitor closet.

"Eric, Geoff," Roy said as he stepped into the foyer.

"Heya Roy," Geoff said.

"Hmph," Eric said, his version of a cordial greeting.

"How's it hanging?"

"Low and knobbly," Geoff said.

"Hmph," Eric said, conveying that the nature of his dangling member was neither relevant nor interesting.

Roy chuckled in solidarity, then hooked the door handle and yanked it open. Clanks and clatters flooded the foyer, along with a fart of machinery steam. Roy slipped inside and the door closed behind him.

The lights softened to a dusky hue, like a swamp cave with an ambient glow. Roy trudged through a short hallway full of blinking lights and pressure gauges. Numerous breaker panels hummed behind panes of clouded glass. Thick bundles of wires drooped overhead. Towards the end, a large red button stuck out from the wall like an infected zit.

Roy smacked the button as he entered the main room.

Everyone pressed the big red button. It was an oddball tradition, like tapping the feet of a campus statue. When The Pipes first opened, nobody pressed the big red button because nobody knew what it did. But then a wobbly drunk accidentally pressed the button. A panic ensued, but nothing happened. From that day on, everyone pressed the big red button.

It served some unknown purpose back in the early days of construction, but the nature of its function had faded over time. Strangely enough, a connection was bridged when the button was pushed. It did *something*, but affected nothing in the immediate area, so that something remained a mystery.

"Roooy," said a chorus of barflies.

"Hey guys," Roy said as he dropped his toolbox along the wall. He hooked his jacket on a valve handle and approached the central bar.

The entire room radiated a workman vibe. Countless pipes and conduits stretched vertically along the walls. Steel, copper, plastic, every feasible housing carried something from somewhere to elsewhere. Valves and wheels of all shapes and sizes peppered the assembly, serving as a giant control hub. The hums and clatters of moving material filled the room with a constant racket. A potent stench of moldy fuel lingered inside like an unwashed vagrant who refused to leave. The chamber seemed to go out of its way to assault every sense with reckless abandon.

Many pipes forked at the ceiling and slithered across the room, creating a zigzagged mosaic overhead. Fiona used them as anchors for decor and lighting. Pub flags and Edison bulbs dangled at random intervals. The bar itself rested at the center and resembled a welded heap plucked from a scrapyard. This was intentional, as anything residing in the pub needed enough resilience to tolerate a vigorous power wash. Thus, a fresh coat of paint was regarded as a needless luxury. Mismatched panels decorated the rectangular frame, and that was good enough. It was a sturdy structure, and as ugly as the patrons surrounding it.

Standard bar fittings littered the rest of the room. A handful of waist-high tables, stools of various sizes, all of it welded for strength. Fiona never lost sight of the place from a practical standpoint. Yes, it was a pub. But it also served a vital purpose. Fiona commanded that purpose from behind the bar, instructing able-bodied patrons to address repairs as needed. That was the price of admission. She ruled with an iron fist and a dirty apron.

Roy plopped onto his favorite stool along the bar, a Norm-like position that he claimed years ago. As one of the primary regulars, the seat vacated as soon as he walked into the room, not that there was ever much clamoring. Duncan and Clancy had already claimed their seats beside him, as per usual. A pair of half-empty mugs rested on the counter.

"Evening, gents," Roy said.

"Howdy," Duncan said with a wide smile.

"About time," Clancy said. "Where the hell you been?"

"Shove it, haircut. I'm like a minute late."

"Yeah, and that's a big deal for you. How many times have you chastised us for not being on time? You say 'eight means eight' like a fucking brain tick."

"Fair enough. Got into another scuffle."

Duncan chuckled. "Did you go all frothy loony?"

"Yup. Fucker turned tail like a frightened child."

"What sparked it?" Clancy said and took another sip.

"Stupid shit. Got checked by a meathead and I checked him back."

Clancy smirked and nodded. "Few things sweeter than owning a bully."

"Says the asshole foreman."

"Hey, I get paid to be a bully. Difference."

A frosty mug of beer clunked in front of Roy, compliments of a smiling Fiona. "There you go, sweetie."

"Ah, thank you, Fifi." He snatched the grog and raised it to his chums.

They raised their own in response.

"To the horses," Roy said with confidence.

The toast paused in mid-air.

"Huh?" Duncan said.

"What, like cowboy horses?" Fiona said.

"The fuck is a cowboy?" Clancy said.

"I don't get the context," Duncan said through a vexed expression.

Roy sighed. "Jeez, nevermind. I heard it somewhere and thought it sounded cool. Fuckin' cheers, you uncultured pricks."

"Cheers," they said in unison and clinked glasses.

Roy took a long swig, then nodded and smacked his lips. "Not bad."

"Got it in this morning," Fiona said while leaning on the counter. "Small batch, strong and malty. It's been quite popular, so get your fill while you can. Third tap from the left."

"Noted," Roy said as he eyed the unlabeled tapline.

Fiona click-winked and turned her attention to a waving patron.

Part of the *free beer for free work* deal involved a stipulation on quality. The inherent nature of such a deal attracted a certain breed of clientele, the kind unburdened by flavors and nuance. Therefore, Durangoni decreed that any beers delivered must adhere to a certain character, or lack thereof. Countless breweries called the station home, everything from tiny brewpubs to massive corporate outfits. The Pipes usually received a steady supply of macro overstock. But every now and then, an "off" batch from a brewpub got added to the mix. A rare treat for the peasants, and one that didn't last long.

Roy palmed his mug and sank into his seat. He released a heavy sigh as Duncan blathered on about something he believed to be interesting, which was rarely interesting. Roy just stared at his mug and nodded along, like a tired parent suffering through a teenage rant. He kept nodding long after Duncan had finished.

"You okay there, Roy?" Clancy said.

Roy kept nodding.

Duncan nudged his shoulder.

Roy flinched and cleared his throat. "Oh, um ... sorry."

Clancy angled himself towards Roy and rested an elbow on the counter. "What's wrong with you today?"

"Nothing."

"Malarkey," Duncan said. "You've been a Negative Nelly all day."

"More than usual," Clancy said. "Seriously, what's wrong?"

Roy sighed and tapped his mug. "It's just, the whole thing is one giant reminder of how stupid and dull and worthless my life is. Everything I do is a cleanup. Everything I am is an afterthought of something else."

"That's not true," Duncan said, then turned to Clancy for support.

Clancy stammered for some positivity, but eventually threw in the towel. "He ain't wrong."

Duncan gasped and whipped his gaze between the two, cycling through *how dare you* and *don't listen to him.*

"It's okay, Duncan." Roy grimaced and shook his head. "My ex-wife hates me, my children don't know me, and I live in the bowels of a mechanized mega-station in order to support them. I was a goddamn architect back home. Respected. Comfortable. But nooo, that wasn't enough for Greedy McBitcherson. So here I am, a divorced slave to someone else's betterment." He tossed back the remainder of his beer as the other two looked on with concern.

"Well, um ..." Duncan searched for the words, but couldn't find any.

"Could be worse," Clancy said.

Roy narrowed his eyes and turned to Clancy. "Do tell, foreman to the stars."

"What's that supposed to mean?"

"I will never understand why you come here. You are hot enough and rich enough to never set foot in this place. For fuck's sake, you live a thousand levels above the merchant line. Why slum it down in this shithole?"

Clancy shrugged, refusing to take the bait.

Roy grunted and bowed his head. "Sorry."

"No offense taken," Clancy said and finished his brew.

Duncan emptied his lungs, relieved by the diffusion. He downed the rest of his brew and slid the empty mug towards the ledge.

Fiona wandered back and hooked all three mugs with one swoop. She refilled them with a practiced hand and distributed them accordingly, prompting a round of thanks. "Roy, I need a pressure calibration on A113."

"I got it," Clancy said and rose from his stool. He gestured at Fiona, as if to say *Dude needs a break tonight.*

Fiona smiled and nodded back. She patted Roy's hand, then grabbed a rag and moseyed out to wipe some tables.

"How do you do it, Duncan?" Roy said.

"Do what, guy?"

"Be happy. How do you find joy in this pit?"

Duncan thought for a moment while shifting his blubbery jowls. "There's always a worse pit, I suppose."

"Do you not want a better life than this?"

Duncan shrugged. "Never give it much thought, to be honest. I find it's easier to be content where I'm at."

Roy stared at a smiling Duncan. "I can't decide if that's wise or stupid."

"I'm fine either way." He grabbed his mug and took a large gulp.

A half-grin lifted Roy's cheek, then he returned to his own mug. His face went limp as he studied the fading suds. The surrounding racket faded with them, as if sinking into a deep pool. For once, the cold blanket of depression had morphed into something else. Maybe it was the good beer talking, or maybe it was the flink that flarked the plumbo. *

(* Some cultural sayings do not translate well into Earth tongues. In this case, the easiest substitute would be "the straw that broke the camel's back," but this visual fails to capture the intended severity. A more apt comparison would be the final handful of dung dropped into a trebuchet that hurls a sheep into a brick wall. But alas, saying "the final shit that slaughters the sheep" elicits more confusion than understanding.)

CHAPTER 4

To understand Roy, one must understand the loyal regulars that call
The Pipes home. And to understand them, one must understand the
newcomers. First-timers are very easy to spot. Simply look for anyone shouting.

The sheer quantity of noise overwhelming the space rivals most
death metal concerts. As such, new visitors will often feel the need to
exceed the ambient volume when ordering a tasty beverage. However, screaming a drink order is a needless exercise because the bar-
tenders have developed a keen sense of inference, using a mixture of
body language and lip-reading. Most newcomers lose their voice and
never return. But for the brave few, the unspoken reward is a new
and covert form of communication.

Barflies actually converse at normal volumes inside The Pipes.
Granted, they are not discussing the philosophical meanings of
Nurmquashi (the local equivalent of Shakespeare, known for stirring
productions that involve actual stage death). It does not take a whole
lot of brainpower to infer the core meanings behind typical pub
chats. Bad day at work, wife got the fleas, the local leader of whatever
is a total douchebag. In fact, many regulars can enjoy entire conversations using only grunts and shrugs.

So why does this matter in the slightest?

In a word: cameras.

The vast majority of Durangoni is under constant surveillance. Managing a trillion residents inside a planet-sized space station requires a massive security force and a highly sophisticated AI system. Every square inch of public space is monitored around the clock. Private domiciles are technically exempt, but the sheer scale of dominion means that everyone assumes they're being watched anyway. Thankfully, the station does not give two flurming flarps about how residents spend their me-time. They're much more concerned with keeping the station afloat.

The Pipes are also monitored, but the pub is so obnoxious that even the most advanced cameras record little more than choppy static. Sound is disabled because playback would be pointless. Not that they care much, as any criminal in their right mind would never conduct dealings in such a place.

The great irony is that The Pipes were instrumental in the lead-up to The Incident. Thus, learning about this lead-up is nigh impossible without interviewing those who shared regular interactions with Roy. In conducting my own inquiries, I found no one more important than his best friend, a mild-mannered chap named Duncan.

I sat down with Duncan numerous times. The first thing one notices is his jovial demeanor, which can be utterly infectious and wholly disarming. I never heard him complain once about anything or anyone. This is due in large part to the nature of his species, a plump and leathery lot known for their passive take on pretty much everything. They depart the womb with a mind for leisure, content to wander through life with a one-way ticket to anywhere. They are found all over the cosmos, and none of them arrive with any formal plan. They are, in a very orthodox sense, just winging it.

Duncan was no different. He left his home planet as a single gardener, traveled the galaxy as a single gardener, ended up on Durangoni as a single gardener, and currently maintains his status as a single gardener. He is perfectly content with this backstory and is more than happy to regale it when prompted. He lives in a tiny apartment deep inside the sub-core, which he has maintained for over 30 years. This utter devotion to inertia is how he came to meet Roy.

Every discussion I ever had with Duncan took place inside his spartan home. He was always happy to receive me and treated my visits like a pampering grandmother. I was initially skeptical about conducting an interview down in the turbulent sub-core. I thought for sure that the noise would be too distracting. Or at the very least, the inevitable headache would force me to cut the meeting short. But as always, Duncan managed to surprise me.

The following is an excerpt from our first interview.

* * *

I rounded a final corner on my way to Duncan's home, and not a moment too soon. I had experienced rowdy districts before, but the sub-core put them all to shame. It was a ceaseless assault of hums, drums, clanks, and clatters. How anyone could tolerate this turmoil, let alone live inside it, was beyond my comprehension.

I entered a narrow corridor with dim light, musky air, and tarnished paneling. Countless doors littered the passage, like steerage on a starcruiser. Their close proximities foreshadowed the scale of their interiors. One door stood out among the rest, as it was covered with stickers, posters, flags, and various shades of permanent marker. It wasn't Duncan's place, but I would learn through Duncan what it represented.

The apartment I sought was four doors down, another empty pane with etched numbers that matched the ones on my comdev. I gave it a stout knock, assuming the noise would get drowned out. Duncan opened the door right away, always the vigilant host. He donned a wide smile and extended a plump hand with sausage-like fingers. I gripped it, we exchanged pleasantries, and then he ushered me inside.

When the door closed, the room went dreadfully silent, enough to stop me in my tracks as if something were afoul. Duncan chuckled and explained that a combination of special foliage and noise cancelation rendered the space, well ... audibly normal. And indeed, a tangled forest of leaves and vines crawled up the walls and along the ceiling, all of which was lovingly trimmed and pleasantly arranged. In lieu of knick-knacks, he decorated the interior with a cornucopia of potted plants. His love of greenery was on full display. As a result, the air was as crisp and clean as the station surface.

Calling the place a studio apartment would be a tad generous. It was a box. Specifically, a stumpy rectangle that would get uncomfortably crowded with a handful of visitors. Furnishings amounted to a small table, a few cabinets, shelves stuffed with plants, and a plush lounge chair that filled much of the space. The lonely table was adorned with sweet morsels and a steaming pot of tea, a kind gesture considering the cramped confines.

Duncan retrieved a folding chair from beside the table and offered it to me proudly, as if to brag on his ability to receive guests. I accepted it, unfolded it, and took a much-needed seat. He poured himself a cup of tea and plopped his rotund body into the lounge chair, expelling a grunt as he landed. His chubby jowls, tiny eyes, and stumpy ears gave me the distinct impression of a kindly krombaloom (think hippo with an injection of koala cuteness). He grinned and patted the armrests as I started my recorder and placed it on the table.

To start, I wish to thank you for welcoming me into your home. It was a very kind offer and I must admit that I am pleasantly surprised.

You betcha. First time down in the sub-core?

First extended visit, yes.

It's not as bad as they say. It can be a bit brassy, but one can manage just fine.

That's a healthy way to look at it.

A lot of good people call the sub-core home. Yes, many of them are of modest means, but many choose this life, as I have. There's a certain authenticity to it that you can't find anywhere else on the station.

What kind of authenticity?

Well, the folk you meet down here are honest from the get-go. There's no reason to wear a mask because there's no lesser stature to contend with. (chuckles) I mean, who ya gonna impress with all your diddly-do?

Did Roy understand that?

I think he did, even though his presence was largely financial.

Fiona informed me of his situation. I imagine that's a tough spot for anyone.

He was just trying to be a good dad. No shame in that. A lot of subbers work here to support somewhere else. Here's a fun fact: Durangoni generates more wealth than the next thousand solar systems combined. It's why the station is a thriving plentitude of culture. It's a big shiny beacon for anyone looking for a better deal. I have met migrants from clear-cross the cosmos, wide-eyed folk who spent their life savings just to get here. If I had to wager, I would say that a solid two-thirds of the sub-core is made up of working transients.

And that's not a source of animosity?

Why would it be? We're all here for the same reason, so there's dinky-do to fight about. Don't much care if someone talks different or wears a funny hat.

I guess we're all transients inside Durangoni.

(smiles) In a big fake world, everyone is from somewhere else.

The upper tiers hear stories about scuffles in the sub-core. Are those unfounded?

Well, when you cram a bunch of roustabouts into close quarters, there are bound to be some fisticuffs every now and then. Not saying they don't happen, but I imagine they aren't near as sensational as headlines suggest. Take Roy for instance. He had a way of neutralizing scuffles that would scare the dickens out of the average upper.

How so?

Ghost-eyed acid puke.

(awkward silence)

So how did you meet Roy?

Hmm. If memory serves, he moved into the row about eight years back. You actually passed his unit on your way here.

You mean the one with all the flair?

(nods) Yes sir. Roy is a bit of a folk hero these days. His lease is still active, so it just sits there empty. Fans come and go, leaving doodads and whatnot. Tim bless 'em, I hope he's doing well, wherever he may be.

So you have no idea what happened to him?

No one does, far as I reckon. I was his closest friend, so if he wanted to be noticed, I imagine a pop-up here would have been at the top of his list. (sighs) But I haven't seen him since the, um, thinga-ma-doodle.

The Incident.

That's the one. (grins) Sharp fella, you are.

How did you weather the fallout?

Just sat in my chair and waited for it to pass.

Really? Did you not, um ... *see* things?

(widens eyes and slowly nods) Oh yes, it was scary as a mud-rucker. But what could I do? I just rode the freaky deaky like everyone else.

Fair enough. So let's talk more about your friendship with Roy.

How did it start?

Plodders on the same row tend to work together fairly often. Management likes to hire by block whenever possible, makes it easier to monitor tardiness. We came to know each other through odd jobs and the like. Gardening and plumbing tend to crissy-cross, so I spent a lot of time with Roy. I was one of the first regular faces he encountered after moving to Durangoni. He wasn't peculiar by any means, just another grunt in need of a friend.

Fiona said that he didn't talk much about his past. But being his closest friend, did he ever elaborate to you? Not meaning to pry, just trying to understand the launch point.

Totally understand, no fouls afoot. And to answer your question, yes and no. Roy was candid about many things, mostly pertaining to his life aboard the station. He griped about the work, complained about the boss, you know, standard grunt prattle. He would always tie it back to his home plights, but we never learned where that home was. For whatever reason, he guarded that info like a noozipup with a parpalapple. *

(* This saying has never been recorded anywhere else in the known universe. It's a Duncan original, so let's just say a "squirrel with a nut.")

Any guesses as to why?

No idea, to be honest. For most subbers, those stories are what get them through the day. We drink suds and chat about our home-worlds like you drink fancy wine and chat about frilly shoes and whatnot. (raises hands) Meaning no offense.

None taken.

But Roy was different. He carried a grouse about losing dignity, which he blamed on that harpy of a spouse. But again, none of this was verified because nobody knew where he came from. It could have been a flagrant fib for all we knew.

Did you ever ask him directly?

No, never. That's a subber blunder. There's an unspoken rule when chatting about the past. You can ask for more, but only after the course is served.

That explains a lot, actually. When I started delving into the details that led up to The Incident, I learned early on that Roy had never registered a surname or applied for trusts. He maintained a unit account, but all you need for that is a retinal scan. As such, sleuthing out a backstory became nigh impossible. It often feels like I'm chasing a shadow.

None of us did any better, and we *drank* with him.

* * *

The rest of our chat provided no additional insights. Subsequent chats would uncover bits and pieces, as Duncan was always a willing and forthright interviewee. It is perfectly forgivable to overlook obscure details, so I never minded the return visits.

More on that later.

I returned to the surface with a small dose of clarity, but answers to the major questions still eluded me. I was no closer to sussing out a motivation than when I started. In reality, it felt like a step in the opposite direction after learning how evasive Roy had been with his closest ally. In a strange way, he made more sense as a supervillain.

As a parting observation, I would be remiss not to highlight the incredible plant life growing inside Duncan's humble abode. I learned that many were selected for their medicinal properties, some of which required the care and attention of a hospice patient. Duncan is a rare breed in that he possesses an encyclopedic knowledge of interstellar botany, both from cultural and scientific bookends.

Durangoni is home to the largest biodiversity in the entire supercluster, a fact that attracted Duncan to the station. Locals came to view him as a medicine man of sorts, someone to call upon when the standard pharma failed to treat. He also grew a collection of rare herbs and spices that he used to season meals and brew pots of tea. Having sampled much of the latter, I would rank his tiny sub-core home as the single greatest teahouse aboard the station. I am also fully aware that this would send a shockwave through the Definitive Directory of Durangoni, so it remains a personal opinion.

Of all my interviews with Duncan, I cherish the first above the rest. It left me with a better understanding and a deeper appreciation of the hardworking folk who call the sub-core home.

CHAPTER 5

Roy glanced down at his comdev resting on the bar and cringed at the wee morning hour. A return to the gardens was fast approaching, but the weight of depression kept him glued to his barstool. His foggy gaze slogged over to the stools beside him, long empty since Clancy and Duncan departed. A sigh escaped his chest as he surveyed the remaining barflies around The Pipes. Just a handful. A spotted reptilian with stumpy limbs, a transparent blob that jiggled with the ruckus (perhaps it viewed the pub as a cheap spa), and a long-necked creature with a trio of ring marks around its throat.

Roy narrowed his eyes as Fiona filled a mug with dark beer and plunked it in front of the long-necked patron, who sat a few stools down. It nodded and smiled, which Fiona returned in kind. She dried her hands with a shoddy rag and tossed it under the counter. Roy and his soured face caught her eye, reeling her over for a chat.

"What's the matter?" Fiona said.

"I can't believe you serve those filthy creatures."

The alien met eyes with Roy, then looked away in discomfort.

"The hell you talking about?"

"Those fucking ringnecks."

Fiona cocked an eyebrow. "Wow. I never took you for a Bob-hating bigot."

Roy stopped mid-sip and clunked his mug on the counter. "Bob's awesome, I don't hate Bob. Why do you think I hate Bob?"

"You just ragged on ringnecks."

"No, no, he has *two* rings. *Huge* difference."

"*What?* They're the same fucking species, Roy."

"No, numbers matter. I love Bob like a brother, but three rings is an abomination."

Fiona shook her head. "That's a very specific racism."

"Just saying, the station would be a much better place without so many goddamn ringnecks." He glanced at the creature, who replied with a miffed gaze. Roy stiffened his posture and spread his arms. "You wanna go, boy?"

The creature rolled its eyes and turned away.

Fiona grabbed Roy's forearm. "No, none of that shit in here. You know the rules."

"Not gonna do anything, you know that."

"I don't know that, actually. And since I rarely see this side of you, I do not intend to find out."

"Oh c'mon, I—"

"Finish your drink and head home. You're cut off."

Roy stammered, then bowed his head with embarrassment.

Fiona eyed him like a disappointed mother as she stepped away. She offered an apology to the offended, who shrugged it off as drunken idiocy.

Roy, now berated and dejected, tossed back a final sip and clunk-slid his mug to the edge of the counter. He spun out of the stool and hit the floor with a brief stumble. A vomit-burp teased his throat, prompting a wince and swallow. He eyed the exit, then shuffled towards his toolbox. He plucked his jacket from an overhead valve and slipped his arms inside, careful to avoid eye contact with anyone. The stench of shame was palpable. Even the blob had angled its jelly head for a better view. Roy hooked his toolbox and stumbled into the hallway. A limp slap on the big red button concluded his visit.

The journey home was a slog through predictability. Roy wandered back to the train station, boarded a pod, and descended into the sub-core. His dignity seemed to fade with every stop. By the time he arrived at his destination, the pod featured a who's who of dregs and drifters. A ding overhead signaled the end of the line, the deepest that deep goes, at least for someone like Roy. From there, the train would start its long climb back to the surface.

The doors opened and the pod dumped its unwanted cargo. Roy stepped into a station that resembled the inside of a derelict shack, complete with a tattered sofa that no one dared to use. Bits of trash stirred with each gust of dank air. Numerous dents and scratches adorned the drab walls. The train consumed a few new passengers and hurried away, like a minivan fleeing the ghetto. Roy stood inside the dirty station like a mental patient dumped on Skid Row. He sighed, then straggled towards his homeward tunnel.

Roy moseyed through a small maze of dark alleys and side passages. He ducked a steam vent just before it released, a habitual reaction even when drunk. Rounding a final corner, he entered a narrow tunnel with a grated walkway and numerous doors to either side. A wearied brain tallied the passing units before hooking his own handle and yanking it open. He glanced down the hallway to Duncan's abode and paused for a moment. It was late and he knew it, big workday ahead. Hardly the time for a chat, no matter how much he needed it. Roy sighed, then slipped into his crummy apartment.

Curiously, nobody locked their doors in the sub-core. The unspoken assumption was that nobody had anything worth stealing. All currency was virtual and all activities were recorded. Thus, locking a door had precisely the opposite effect. It showed that you harbored something worth taking. Contrary to popular opinion, robberies were exceedingly rare down in the bowels of Durangoni. Most breaches of privacy amounted to new tenants entering the wrong units by mistake, sometimes during a vexing avocation. Instant regret ensured that the correct unit got memorized in a hurry.

Roy stood inside his modest apartment. His tired fingers released the weight of the toolbox, allowing it to clunk onto the hard metal floor. The funk of his own filth nagged his nostrils, now that it could fester inside a confined area. Roy cringed at the sudden awareness, but was too tired and depressed to do anything about it. He just stood there, silent and alone inside what amounted to a cramped storage locker.

Roy never coveted much. He was fond of saying that all he needed was "a place to piss and grub to gobble." A small cooler satisfied the latter, but the former required a long stroll to the communal wash facilities. Sub-core life was simple to the point of shared misery. Roy had since amended his favorite saying with the suffix "in the same place." Heeding the call of nature in a group setting was awkward enough with the same species, let alone in a bathroom full of aliens with conflicting hygiene standards. There was a better than average chance that cleaning oneself meant foraging through a fog of mental, physical, and sensual horror. It was a battle that Roy just couldn't deal with at the moment.

Instead, he shuffled over to a simple cot along the wall and tossed his wearied body on top. His back thumped against the wall, forcing a grunt of exhaustion. The heartbeat of the sub-core surrounded him, from the rattles in the walls to the distant sounds of grinding gears. Roy could only close his eyes and expel a weighted sigh. His troubled mind took stock of its own reality, as it was prone to do from time to time. A lazy gaze wandered the room, uncovering little more than the artifacts of a meager existence. No decorations, just four blank walls with a few dings and scratches. A small stack of boxes leaned against the corner, containing the basics for continued survival. Three wire hangers clung to notches in the wall, serving as an official closet. A handful of frumpish clothes hung from their warped frames.

Roy reached over to a small red cooler beside the cot, i.e. the kitchen, and retrieved a dented canteen filled with lukewarm water. He popped the top and chugged a large portion, initiating the long march back to soberness. The jug found a home beside his leg as he fished the comdev from his pocket. Roy stared at the black mirror in his hand and caught a glimpse of his own disheveled reflection. His brain recoiled in disgust, resulting in another heavy sigh.

"Directory," Roy said with a flat tone.

The device pinged to life and glowed with a pleasant blue sheen. A white "D" appeared on the screen and spread into three distinct letters, the opening sequence to the Definitive Directory of Durangoni. Roy flicked the screen onto the far wall, then dropped the comdev to his side. The room dimmed as a deep blue consumed the space, like his own personal movie theater, but minus the fun and enjoyment. A short melody signaled a readiness to receive command.

"Kink Rinks," Roy said, as he had so many times before.

The directory pinged in response, then displayed a grid of relevant categories. Bold titles hovered above numerous video clips. An outline of the space station floated in the upper corner with the target rings selected.

Roy shifted his lips. "Brothel District 7."

The directory pinged, the grid filtered, and the station image zoomed.

"Celestial Seraphs."

Ping, filter, zoom. A selection of scantily clad aliens filled the wall.

Roy scanned the options, then grinned. "Elora."

The directory pinged and the grid faded, revealing an erotic creature with cherry-red skin, luscious lips, and striking pink eyes. She swayed her hips and winked with naughty intent. Every so often, she would kiss her palm and blow through her fingers, prompting hearts and ribbons to swirl around her body.

"Schedule."

A calendar popped up beside the image with available dates blinking.

Roy opened his mouth, but paused. A sudden and crippling sadness infected him. He bowed his head as his eyes began to water. Whimpers built inside his chest and clawed their way to the surface. Tears rolled down his cheeks and dripped onto his dirty shirt, turning spots of grime into salty mud. Despite having every reason in the world, he refused to wail. He just sat upon his cot, slumped and alone, weeping in silence.

The directory pinged and suggested a psychiatrist. Or rather, a prostitute dressed like a psychiatrist. (Many customers conflated the two.)

Roy took offense and tossed his canteen at the wall. The impact sprayed some water across the image, giving it a moist sheen that seemed like overkill. The canteen clanked to a rest on the floor. Roy concluded the outburst with a rude gesture.

The directory pinged and suggested a dominatrix. And not just any whip-toting harlot, this vixen wore a full gimp suit with deep red eyes that screamed pain. The upper arms cracked a studded whip while the lower arms thumped a leathery bat. Her firm breasts refused to move inside their skin-tight confines. The thick trunks below her waist seemed well-suited for an Olympic track event.

Roy shuddered as a scheduling calendar popped up. Much to his surprise, the mistress was booked solid, but she was kind enough to offer Roy a cancellation slot. His brain considered it for a split second, then remembered that it frowned on torture.

"Reset! Reset. Please reset."

The directory pinged and returned to its default state.

Roy stared at the three white D's floating on the blue backdrop. His mind descended into a dark yet comfortable place, far away from the cold realities of everyday life. Time lost meaning as the tug of responsibility faded from reality. His breathing slowed, like a plump bear prepping for hibernation. He slumped against the rear wall like a gunshot victim awaiting the sweet release of death. After a spell of intense yet involuntary meditation, Roy filled his lungs with the stale air of poverty and exhaled a sigh of fortitude.

"Monger District, Northern Ring."

The directory pinged, filtered, and zoomed to an area just below the Kink Rinks. A listing of specialty services filled the wall, everything from bootleggers to exotic traders.

Roy squinted as he scanned the options. "Extractions."

Ping, filter, zoom.

Roy cringed at a selection of mercenary outfits and non-network dentists. "Back."

41

The directory complied.

"Um ... the Underminer Network."

Ping, filter, zoom. Another list of unsettling options.

"Back."

The directory complied.

Roy sighed and rubbed his face with both hands. "Okay, let's try something different. Reset and open a conceptual search."

The directory pinged and wiped clean. A lonely cursor blinked in the upper corner.

Roy bowed his head and thought for a while, allowing a collection of seldom-uttered words to organize themselves. "Excitement."

The word appeared on the search screen.

"Danger."

The directory appended the list.

"Seductive. Thrilling. Provocative. Extreme."

The list appended each term.

Roy grinned as he studied the input. "Search."

After a short churn, the same dominatrix appeared on the screen. "Dammit." Roy grunted with frustration. "Reset."

The directory complied.

Roy plunked his head against the rear wall and closed his eyes. "All I want is a break. An actual break from the never-ending bullshit. This life, this fucking life. I want to do something, see something, be part of something, anything, anything with actual consequence. Something that matters to somebody else. Not for money, not for fame, not for the greater good, whatever the fuck that means. I just want to feel something other than regret when I wake up. I want to sleep without hating every second of the day. Is that too much to ask?"

He huffed with chagrin, then lifted his eyelids. Much to his surprise, the directory had recorded his every word into the search field. A blinking cursor hung at the end of a woeful monologue. Roy reread his own words with a steady and deliberate eye. The weight of every letter settled upon his shoulders. His gut twisted with self-pity. While staring at the cursor, he allowed a single word to escape his lips. "Search."

The directory complied.

After a long churn, it returned a single name.

Roy studied the bio of a larger-than-life character, a scoundrel of sorts with a legendary reputation. It seemed fictitious beyond words, like the profile of an *Indiana Jones* villain. But the name rang true, at least to anyone who had ever gossiped inside Durangoni. The entry offered no calendar, no schedule, only a simple message option.

"New message," Roy said with a stomach full of butterflies.

* * *

Roy awoke several hours later, having gotten less than adequate sleep. In fact, the sleep had been downright shitty, partly due to a throbbing hangover, but mostly due to the intense anxiety over sending an unsolicited message to a fearsome thug. Perhaps an unfounded anxiety, as Roy wasn't the most formidable of assets. A damn good plumber, but a warrior he was not.

He grabbed his comdev from atop the cooler and hesitated before powering it on, like a teenager awaiting a reply from a crush. But alas, no messages. He sighed and plunked the device back onto the cooler.

Roy lifted his aching body from the cot and swung his feet to the floor. A pungent aroma began to tease his nostrils, the unfortunate result of forgoing a shower the previous evening. He had slept in his own funk and went so far as to infect the cot. Thus, a deep and thorough cleaning of his tiny abode climbed to the top of his to-do list. He winced at the inescapable odor, but took solace in the fact that he didn't need to dress for work.

Tired joints cracked and popped as he rose from the bed, drawing a grunt and grimace. A quick scan of the interior uncovered the usual dullness, along with a toppled canteen resting in a small puddle of water. He shuffled over to the puddle, plucked the container from the floor, and finished off the remaining water inside. A sudden need to pee captured his attention, cueing the start of a typical day.

The morning routines for sub-core folk were largely similar. After rousing under a blanket of noise, they emerged from their tiny abodes and stumbled towards the communal wash. A chorus of groans filled the space as residents emptied bowels and prepped for a new day. For once, Roy was a major source of nasal discomfort, but at least the visit would be brief.

The facilities were a menagerie of tiled booths, ceiling faucets, floor drains, shitting holes, and pissing troughs. A constant flow of recycled water entered the space through every faucet and exited through every drain. You simply walked inside, did your business, then got the hell out before things got weird. Despite the constant traffic, the washrooms were not social places. They functioned more like assembly lines with a steady flow from start to finish. There was no privacy, nor qualms about its absence. Modesty is a non-issue when everyone has different parts, different habits, and different hang-ups about said parts and habits.

Roy wandered through a doorless portal and searched for a free space along the troughs. He proceeded to empty his bladder while trying to ignore the disgusting sounds of numerous aliens answering the call of nature. A particularly loud plop and moan forced his brain to contemplate a turn and look. Luckily, his brain locked his neck in place and settled for a cringe.

Roy shook once, shook twice, then crashed his forehead into the tile wall. To be fair, the last part wasn't voluntary. After a sharp yelp and a bout of dizziness, Roy turned to find three naked ringnecks staring him down. The horse-like humanoids stood tall with their arms crossed and massive cocks dangling like grandfather clocks. Three rings encircled each of their long necks, guaranteeing an unpleasant experience for Roy. Without missing a beat, his eyes glazed over as stomach acid began to boil. And without missing the next beat, one of the ringnecks bashed him across the cheek, bringing the defensive trick to a sudden halt. Roy stumbled backwards into the trough, splashing piss as he fell. A room full of naked aliens turned to watch, leaving the whine of water pipes to cut the tension.

"So I hear you don't like ringnecks," one of the ringnecks said.

Roy scanned the room for an out, but found a wall of eyes and swinging willies. A beating for sure, so might as well commit. He locked eyes with the obvious leader and spat at his feet. "Only tri-ring fucks like you and your girlfriends."

The ringneck smirked. "This isn't going to end well for you."

Roy shrugged. "Never does."

The brute hooked Roy by the collar and hurled him across the washroom. He sailed through several water jets on his way to the floor, rinsing away some of the piss. The crowd parted as Roy hit the ground and slid into the far wall. The impact forced a grunt from his throat as he settled facedown in the dirty water.

The ringnecks sauntered across the room with their third legs slapping against their thighs. The leader grinned before burying his foot into Roy's flank. Roy yelped as the others followed suit. They kicked the shit out of him, despite already swimming in a sea of actual shit. One of the ringnecks reared back for another blow, but then shrieked with sudden pain. The other two spun around to find Duncan standing behind them with a death grip on the other's cock.

"Howdy fellas," Duncan said with his usual upbeat tone. He waved with one hand and jerked the other, prompting another shriek.

The victim crumpled to his knees and pinched his eyes shut.

Duncan maintained a vise-like grip as he addressed the other two. "So whatcha doing?"

The leader traded glances between Duncan, Roy, and his suffering sidekick. "Teaching this fool a lesson," he said, gesturing to Roy.

"About what?"

"About being a hateful bigot."

Duncan chuckled and squeezed tighter, drawing a high-pitched squeal. "So you beat on 'em to make 'em hate you less?"

The leader started to respond, but huffed instead.

"For Tim's sake, we live in the sub-core. We all irk someone for some reason, but we smile and nod like civil folk." Duncan turned to his trembling victim. "Wouldn't you agree?" he said, then tugged his tether.

The ringneck swallowed a yelp, gritted his teeth, and hastily nodded.

Duncan smiled. "See? We're all friends here."

The other two traded glances, then softened their stances.

"So if you would be so kind," Duncan said, "help him up and make your peace."

The leader sighed and turned to Roy, who was busy spitting and grousing while rising from the floor muck. The ringneck hooked Roy's arm and yanked him to his feet, drawing a groan and grimace.

"Now give 'em a kiss," Duncan said.

The leader whipped a rattled gaze to Duncan, who laughed in response.

"Just messing with you, friend. We all enjoy a good ribbing. You're free to go, and take this whiny doofus with you." He released his grip and the ringneck collapsed onto the floor, cradling his reddened meat sword.

The other two helped him up and they exited the washroom.

With the excitement over, the crowd returned to their morning routines.

Roy limped over to Duncan and palmed his shoulder. "Thanks, bud."

Duncan winced. "Jeez, you smell ripe. And you're welcome. Care to tell me what that was all about?"

"I may have, um, ranted a bit at The Pipes last night."

"About ringnecks? I thought you liked Bob."

"No, um. I mean yes. I love Bob. I just don't, um—" Roy sighed. "Nevermind."

"Anyhoo, I'm gonna wash up and head to the worksite. You on your way?"

"I was, before getting jumped in the shower. Fuck me, as if this place doesn't resemble a prison enough."

"If you want to wait a tick, we can head up together."

Roy battled a burning desire to flee the washroom, to escape his wounded pride. On the flip side, he also heeded a desire to keep his ass unkicked. His gaze wandered an arena oozing with embarrassment, catching a few glances of pity. Shame flooded his mind, but he refused to show it. He turned to his friend and nodded. "Works for me."

"Okie dokie, won't take long. Just gotta scrub the nethers." Duncan waddled beneath the nearest water jet and released a moan of contentment.

Roy grinned, then glanced down to his soggy clothes. "May as well get a proper rinse." He stripped out of his duds, tossed them aside, and joined his naked brethren.

CHAPTER 6

Clancy Monto Von Schlupnick XLII is the kind of man that women crave and every other man wants to be. Anyone who has ever set foot inside Durangoni has seen his family crest (yes, *those* Von Schlupnicks). This illustrious house has maintained seats of power aboard the station for over 20 generations. While they control an array of business interests, their primary claim to fame continues to be their paper empire. To put it bluntly, wiping your bum with a roll of Von Schlupnick is like wiping with a cloud of virgin kisses. Superior would be an understatement. Von Schlupnick *is* paper.

The unrivaled quality of VS products sets the family apart in ways that need no competitive reinforcement. While they maintain a powerful monopoly, they are also one of the most trusted brands within the station. The Von Schlupnick Society fosters more charities than the next 100 factions combined. Greed is not part of their vocabulary. They worry about power and wealth in the same way that ants worry about dirt. They're awash in it, which allows them to concentrate on philanthropy. In fact, they bring so much good to the station that residents regard them more as benevolent deities.

Clancy grew up in a lap of unimaginable luxury, but he never cared much about it. He has the rugged good looks to grace the cover of Glam Goni (the Durangoni equivalent of Haxfrong Zop Zop on Galwock 36 or GQ on Earth). His lemon-yellow eyes and luscious red lips are the envy of anyone with a pulse. A firm and chiseled body rests beneath a layer of silken fur, giving him the presence of a fleecy gladiator. But despite all of his visual and financial advantages, Clancy prefers the grunt life. He likes to work with his hands and have normal conversations that don't involve undertones of privilege. At a baseline, he's just a regular dude.

Be that as it may, the weight of his family name follows him wherever he goes. An aura of celebrity surrounds him at all times, and even if someone doesn't recognize the inherent status, his attractiveness steps up to fill the void. Clancy takes it all in stride. He views it as more of a mild irritation than a significant problem.

This easygoing attitude is what introduced him to Roy.

I sat down with Clancy several times during my research. What struck me immediately was his complete detachment from entitlement. He's a walking enigma, like someone laser-focused on the little things with a winning lottery ticket in his pocket. The following is an excerpt from our first meeting.

* * *

Clancy had constructed a small interview niche inside his Von Schlupnick condo, one of the countless units across the station. It was a modest place near the service line, featuring tasteful decor with a distinct lack of ostentation. If I hadn't known any better, I would have assumed the abode was soundly middle-class.

He settled across from me in one of two cozy chairs. A snazzy vest, of which he had a vast collection, hugged his burly chest. While clothing was certainly optional for his species, pockets remained a necessity. He crossed his legs and leaned back into the soft cushion, prepping for a relaxing chinwag. Heeding the cue, I started my recorder and set it on the table beside me. We traded smiles as I battled a sudden wave of resentment.

Goddamn you're handsome.

Well, that's one way to start an interview.

No, seriously. It's comically absurd.

Thanks.

Your life must be haunted by hungry gazes.

(shrugs)

But anyway, we're not here to discuss your stupidly amazing genes. It just needed to be addressed, lest it linger in the air like an elevator fart.

(chuckles) Fair enough.

As a Von Schlupnick, you grew up inside a bubble of immense wealth and prosperity. And yet, for the most part, you choose to reject that lifestyle. Why?

I wouldn't say that I reject it. I often get misrepresented as some sort of "fight the power" guy, but that's not it at all. Some view me as a spoiled rich kid that somehow broke free of the upper crust, as if my family was forcing me to attend fancy parties against my will. I enjoy nice things. I just don't covet them. I am equally happy with grunt grog and expensive brandy. I don't chastise the uppers, or anyone else for that matter. It's just not a life that appeals to me.

So you never viewed yourself as a spoiled kid?

Of course I was a spoiled kid. Every brat with food in their belly is a spoiled kid.

That's a bit harsh, don't you think?

Let me rephrase. Every kid understands the concept of starvation. Being hungry is a terrible thing. But no kid understands the mechanism of class dynamics. My cousin exemplifies this perception. In fact, I can better illustrate it with a story.

My family owns an obscene amount of real estate aboard the station, much of which is rented by other prominent families. My cousin lives in a massive beach estate on a central ocean ring, one of the most expensive properties in the entire quadrant. We're talking thousands of rooms over millions of square feet, which takes a small army of servants and maintenance personnel just to keep it functional. And that's for a family of *six*.

My cousin and I are the same age. I visited that property many times growing up because our parents are close and we often played together. The adults would dine on posh cuisine prepared by personal chefs while drinking bottles of wine that cost more than most people make in their lifetimes. But all my cousin and I cared about was the temperature of the pool. We got more joy out of splashing each other than the adults got from sipping that wine.

But anyway, my parents are more reserved when it comes to matters of opulence. We are still supremely wealthy, but flaunting isn't something they care for. Our primary home is a sub-level condo about a mile below my cousin's surface estate. It's about 50,000 square feet with a small service staff, much easier to maintain.

My cousin loved to visit. Not to gloat or tease, but to revel in the simplicity. This was a kid who griped about having to walk a quarter-mile between the home theater and his bedroom, and that's without ever leaving the property. He loved the fact that he could wander anywhere in our home and never get lost. That's kid thinking. He couldn't give two shits about the paintings or the floor tile. He just liked that he could find the kitchen.

And you carried that attitude into adulthood.

In a way. I understand the pros and cons of class. I just like being close to the kitchen.

The place we're in now is more luxurious than most people could ever hope for.

My parents would consider it a closet. My cousin's parents would consider it a drawer.

I guess it's all about perspective.

(nods)

Speaking of perspective, tell me how you acquired a taste for grunt work.

I wouldn't say that I acquired it, per se. It's always been there, just in different forms. Even as a kid, I was more interested in *doing* things than *having* things. As a teenager, that meant clubbing and partying and traveling and whatnot. But as an adult, it's all about learning new skills.

The family business is more or less automated at this point, so there's not much for me to do there. I have always enjoyed learning how things work. I was the kind of kid who dismantled toys to study the insides, much to the annoyance of my parents. And what bigger toy than the Durangoni Space Station? I know it's strange to say, but I love working in maintenance. And since I don't need the money, I feel like a surgeon fixing guts. It's really cool.

Even though robots do the most important work?

As they should. Have you ever been to the inner core?

No, can't say that I have.

I have. It's one thing to watch a video or listen to stories, but it's a whole other thing to see the heart beating in real-time. Those engineers are gods. Even if I could work on a system like that, I would much rather it be handled by the AI. I could spend my entire life learning how a tiny piece of it works, and still not fully grasp it.

You hit on an important yet seldom seen perspective. The sheer complexity of Durangoni, the core specifically, has been blamed for the unfortunate length of The Incident. The chaos that it generated was harrowing for the general population. But

**given the isolated nature of the upper class, how did the afflu-
ent weather the fallout?**

(shrugs) Same as everyone else, I suppose. Power and privilege don't
combat something like that. We just had better homes in which to
suffer, not that it mattered much. I was in the general population
when it happened, spent most of The Incident below the merchant
line. I was hunting for a machine part when the first wave hit.

That had to have been ... interesting.

Yeah. Imagine what you experienced, only surrounded by robo-guts
and sub-core ruckus.

Wow.

Exactly.

**Which, somewhat ironically, brings us to the root of this dis-
cussion. How did you meet Roy?**

I worked on a big project with him many years ago. One of those
major development gigs, station-funded, months of hard work with
massive crews. That's actually how I broke into the industry. It took
me a long time to get regular work because the grunts dismissed me
as a tourist. You know, rich boy slumming it for some misplaced al-
truism. However, I assume you've met Duncan at this point.

(I smile and nod.) Yes.

That pudgy sombitch commands more respect than most CEOs. The
companies fear him, the unions fear him, the politicians fear him, and
yet, he's just a gardener. Duncan is regarded as a gatekeeper of sorts.
If you can get his seal of approval, then you are instantly accepted
into that world. I think he understood my intent and took offense at
my ostracization. He befriended me, as he did with Roy.

Were you three close from the start?

Not really. It took a while to build that rapport. Roy and Duncan were friends first. Roy was the guy who always needed emotional support, but would never admit to it. Duncan, being the father figure type, was always happy to provide it. They had a feedback loop that never ended, and they were both okay with it.

I had casual friends and such, basically chat buddies with no real depth. Roy and Duncan were my first real friends down in the sub-core. Roy was fond of saying that I was the most grounded up-fuck on the station. He goaded me like any friend does, but he always showed me a baseline of respect and never asked for material help. I think he just enjoyed being around someone who didn't have to struggle, to provide that flicker of hope he so desperately needed.

Do you think that desperation pushed him to do what he did?

(ponders for a moment) Perhaps.

You don't sound convinced.

Roy was an odd bird. That's undeniable, even from his inner circle. I considered him a brother before The Incident, which holds true today. I was as surprised as anyone to hear that he played such a big role. I haven't seen or heard from him since that day he left the worksite.

* * *

Roy stood in the same fountain that he had departed the previous day. One hand clutched a wrench while the other tapped his thigh. The filter hummed beneath his feet as he listened for anything abnormal. After a few minutes of studying the rippling water like a meditating monk, he nodded with approval and sloshed back to the ledge. He tossed the wrench into his toolbox and plopped on the fountain rim to remove his waders. A knock to the access hatch clanked it shut, concluding the fix.

Clancy strolled up to the fountain with a tablet in hand. "What's the count?"

"Fuck off, bossman."

Clancy rolled his eyes. "Just gimme the count, Roy."

Roy glanced around the garden space while running a mental tally. "This was eight, which means I have four to go."

"Damn, dude. You're crushing it. Nice work."

"Well, it finally dawned on me that they're all indie systems governed by a master router, which makes servicing more linear. Kinda like fixing a light switch without having to kill the breakers. Pretty slick, to be honest. My compliments to the chef."

"At this rate, you'll be wrapped up later today."

"Probably."

"You got all week, so why not relax and milk some overtime?"

Roy glanced up to the exploded terrace where a crew had started to rebuild the framing. He sighed and turned back to Clancy. "Thanks, but I'd rather be done with it."

"Suit yourself, but there's plenty more on the docket if you want to keep busy."

Roy nodded, then rose into a shoulder stretch.

"I'll take some more diddles," Duncan said as he waddled up.

Clancy sneered in response. "You haven't even finished the fern gully."

"It's a delicate process. Those nubbins need tender lovin'."

"Then love 'em faster. You've still got the rompum beds to repair."

"Oh fiddle poop. Nothin' a good weed-bleeder and bone saw won't fix."

Clancy narrowed his eyes and wondered if he should be concerned.

Roy grinned as Duncan and Clancy continued their peculiar argument. He twisted his torso from side to side to relieve some soreness, letting the conversation fade into the background. His gaze wandered the room, surveying the rehab. Saws and hammers echoed around the interior as new wood panels replaced their splintered kin. Fresh foliage was returning by the truckload. The space was healing, much to Roy's chagrin.

And then his comdev pinged from atop the toolbox.

Duncan and Clancy kept chatting as Roy scooped the device without thinking. He glanced down to find the notice of a new message. His eyes widened as an immediate dread crawled up his spine. The entire room faded as he gawked at the tiny white envelope. His trembling finger floated across the screen and tapped the icon, opening the message.

"Well that's just silly," Duncan said, then turned to Roy. "Doncha think?"

Roy stood there in silence, staring at his phone.

"You okay there, Roy?"

No response.

Clancy ruffled his brow. "Yo, Roy. What's wrong?"

Roy snapped out of his trance with a sharp flinch. He stammered like a frightened child while trading glances between the two. His widened gaze locked onto Clancy as fluttering breaths fled his chest. "I, um ... I have to go."

"Go where?" Duncan said.

Clancy offered a slow nod as he weighed the situation. He studied Roy with a mixture of pity and understanding. After a tense silence, he smirked and sighed. "Then go."

Roy glanced at Duncan, then hurried away without another word.

"What the doodle—" Duncan whipped his gaze between the two, tossing neck fat from ear to ear. "What in the dickens just happened?"

Clancy watched in silence as Roy disappeared into a service tunnel.

* * *

(staring at the floor) That was the last time I saw him.

Did you ever find out what the message was?

No, but I didn't need to. I've seen that look before. I've been around too many schemers to know when a game-changing opportunity presents itself. That was his shot.

To do what?

To fix whatever was broken, for better or for worse. It's debatable as to whether he understood the consequences, but I doubt he did. Roy was never smug or malicious. At least, no more than the average grunt. I could only assume that he had found an escape hatch.

To where?

(shrugs and smirks) Anywhere.

CHAPTER 7

When an asshole gets an idea, it's rarely a good thing for anyone within shitting distance. More often than not, the asshole gets kicked in the teeth and paints the room with feces, leaving everyone around them with a horrible taste and a hefty cleaning bill. Should it not be obvious at this point, I am comparing Roy to a giant asshole.

As I plowed through my research on The Incident, it became more and more apparent that the general public was less and less informed. Roy was a hero to them, for whatever baffling reason. It's not like he Robin Hooded through the station and filled everyone's credit account. Quite the opposite. The public paid dearly for his deeds through mental and financial hardship. And yet, no one seemed to care.

Puki Horpocket cared.

Puki Horpocket wanted answers.

My quest for said answers took me on quite the tour of the space station. With the help of various locals, I visited several places that I never would have found on my own. Yes, even as a distinguished editor for the Definitive Directory of Durangoni. It would seem that my all-access pass had granted me access to diddly-squat.

Roy had served as a decent tour guide, despite his lack of physical presence. Fiona, Duncan, and Clancy had provided crucial insights into Roy the struggling father. I had loosened the knot, but in order to unravel it, I needed insights into Roy the bumbling crook. The path was apparent, but plunging those depths required more than trunks and a snorkel. I needed gainful access to the station's most notorious trafficker.

As an interesting side note, my research never uncovered the message that Roy received in the garden. Comdev services are technically forbidden from recording chat logs, giving them a wall of deniability. Roy never forwarded the message or backed up his data. He was also careful to guard the message in public, as if watching porn on the subway. Thus, it was never revealed to security footage. I could only study him as he studied the message.

But as with any mystery, digging deeper reveals the truth. At the very least, I would learn *who* sent the message and *why* it was sent.

* * *

Roy tore through the crowded tunnels as if competing in the 100-meter push and shove. He racked up more insults and crude gestures than a brombo shuttle slag (the local equivalent of a New York taxi driver). Not that he cared much, as his brain was laser-focused on a sudden sprint to the Rich Rings. Not the most inspired of labels, but it got right to the point. The Central Rings housed most of the commerce while the adjacent Rich Rings housed most of the wealth. Credits flowed freely between them.

Roy arrived at the nearest pod station as an express connector was loading. He shoved his way aboard and received plenty of curses and sour looks. A hologram map glowed overhead, highlighting the current station and the next several stops. The map zoomed out as the train departed, allowing Roy to plot the necessary connections. His racing mind manifested as rapid mumbles and finger-pointing, like a cult leader speaking in tongues. Several passengers hugged their bags and recoiled. Roy glanced around the pod and offered a sheepish smile to the worried eyes staring back at him.

A ping sounded overhead, signaling that the rear pods were about to break away from the train. Access doors allowed riders to shuffle around as needed. Roy snaked his way to the back and settled inside a unit bound for the sub-chutes. Moments later, the pod split from the train and dove deeper into the station. After several twists and turns, it picked up speed and merged into an express tunnel en route to the next ring.

Lighting panels zipped overhead as the pod melded into a northbound train. Roy knew the route well as a Kink Rinks regular. But this time around, a nervous apprehension had replaced his usual cloud of depression. He glanced around at his pod mates, a collection of random faces on their way to nowhere. A strange realization drew an unexpected smile. For once, he was the most interesting person in the pod.

The train sliced through a vacuum barrier and into open space. Or rather, the empty space between rings. Time seemed to slow as the colossal walls of the central rings climbed into the atmosphere far above. Massive pipelines snaked from the core like blood vessels, gifting life to Durangoni. Roy lifted his gaze to the heavens where sunlight poured into the breach, painting the drab metal with a bright yellow sheen. Countless ships of all sizes floated through the beams like motes of dust. Roy marveled at the view, one he hadn't seen in months. It always rang as distant and foreign as the people it represented.

But not today.

This time, he sensed an invitation.

And with a blink, it was gone.

The train punched through the next barrier and into the adjacent ring, refilling the pod with pulses of passing light. Roy sighed and lowered his gaze to the floor, content to pass the time in his own headspace.

The remainder of the journey morphed into a restless slog. Roy double-checked his course with every ping, but even so, he almost missed a crucial split. A sudden panic yanked him to an adjacent pod just before the doors closed. He made it, but his heart began to race with the train. As his destination approached, he fidgeted like an excitable toddler. The official ping of arrival forced a cold chill down his spine.

"Am I really doing this?" he said to nobody.

"Huh?" said a voice beside him.

Roy turned to find a stylish teen with long hair and a limp expression. The image caught him off-guard, forcing him to realize that the onboard clientele had drastically changed. Roy glanced around a cabin filled with shopping bags, swank attire, and glittering jewelry. He could sense an air of intrusion, like a redneck at an opera. Several leery eyes stared back at him.

Roy frowned and returned his gaze to the teen. "Nothing."

"Miss your stop?"

Roy opened his mouth to respond in snark, but paused to appreciate the boy's naive honesty. He sighed instead. "Yes."

"That sucks."

"Ah well, misses happen."

"Truth. Safe journeys, bro."

"You too ... bro."

Roy cracked an actual smile. It was the most pleasant conversation he'd had in months, all by way of a random rich kid. Maybe there was hope for the world after all. But not really. The crush of misanthropy quickly returned to invert the errant smile.

The pod train slowed to a stop. As the doors opened, a rush of perfumed air caused Roy to cringe. Not out of disgust, but from pure surprise. He was so used to the sub-core funk that an actual floral scent confused his brain. His legs locked into place as he cycled through memories of what green things smelled like. After a brief loiter, a throat clear from behind jolted him back to attention. He waved an apology and stepped out onto the station platform.

The sight before him flooded his mind with awe. He paused inside a pocket of traffic to admire the sophisticated nature of life in the Rich Rings. Elegant chandeliers hovered along the ceiling, emitting the ethereal tones of heavenly bodies. Sleek kiosks promoted posh doodads and luxury getaways. Sculpted panels covered the walls and ceiling, the life's work of some forgotten master. Ritzy locals wandered by as if it wasn't the most breathtaking artistry they had ever seen. And of course it wasn't. Roy hadn't even left the train depot yet.

He double-checked his comdev and zeroed in on the appropriate tunnel. Hologram signs and directional colors made the task much easier, a notable improvement over the crude etchings he was used to. He merged into the flow of traffic and prepped his brain for an onslaught of visual stimulus. Sure enough, the tunnel ended at a vast bazaar bursting with opulence. Every boutique housed more retail value than his entire sub-core sect combined. It was a staggering amount of wealth in a concentrated area, something his brain couldn't quite process. With mouth agape, he gazed around one bazaar of one sector of one level of one ring.

With his comdev outstretched, he wandered towards a far tunnel and repeated the process through another series of ritz-marts. Soon after, he ducked behind a specific kiosk and slipped into a narrow service tunnel. Dim lights passed overhead as he crept through the corridor. He strolled beneath a final arch to arrive at his destination.

Or rather, the secluded square that housed his destination.

He glanced around a small pocket of modest pubs, serving as a break area for rich shoppers in need of a cheap drink, but without being seen. Hand-painted signs and dark wood exteriors gave him a fleeting sense of comfort.

And there it was, The Craven Compass, a small pub with a plain badge hanging over the entrance. The perfect place for an illicit affair. Roy closed his eyes, argued with his brain for a moment, then gathered his wits and stepped towards the door.

Roy flinched as a sharp ringing sound greeted his entry. He glanced overhead to find a brass bell attached to the wooden frame. Given the nature of the locale, he rather admired the primitive charm. His gaze fell into a hazy interior that radiated passé. Nothing fancy, nothing garish, just simple forms and pleasant patterns. A cramped dining area surrounded the central bar, where a handful of patrons filled a limited number of stools. They all ignored him, content to nurse their suds in silence. Soft jazz played in the background, loud enough to be noticed, but removed from conversation. A single bartender glanced up while drying a mug with a hand towel.

Roy steadied his breath and stepped towards the bar. He gripped the back of a stool, but did not take a seat. The bartender was a slender chap with green skin, thin lips, and a sharply forked nose that doubled as a mustache. He eyed Roy with mild distaste before lifting his brow, asking *Can I help you?* with the least possible effort.

"I would like ..." Roy paused for thought. "A single-malt Matrondin with two cubes."

The bartender looked him up and down without moving his head, then reached beneath the counter and pressed a hidden button. Soon after, a brutish fellow in slick attire emerged from a side door. Without a word, he glared at Roy and motioned to follow. Roy gulped, then tailed the bloke through the rear kitchen. A sole cook with a bloodstained apron paid them no mind. He smoked a cigarette while handling an agitated snoodlecock. The colorful bird squawked as they passed, startling Roy into a hanging pot. He quelled the resulting bong and muttered an apology to the cook, who continued to deny his existence.

The brute exited the kitchen with Roy in tow and proceeded down a dim hallway. He strolled to a stop at an unmarked door, one of many along the passage. He knocked twice, listened for a faint reply, then gripped the knob and turned to Roy. The hinges whined as the door swung open. Roy took a deep breath and stepped inside.

A hairy beast in a gaudy leisure suit sat behind a large wooden desk. It chewed on a plump cigar, needling the air with wet smacks. A pair of stumpy horns poked through a mane of brown fur. Large red eyes gazed over a bovine-like snout. Thick forearms with meaty paws rested atop the desk, a smooth plane with minimal clutter. A reptilian minion with purple scales and slitted yellow eyes stood behind the beast. It wore black slacks with polished shoes and a button shirt, creating the unsettling image of a serpentine accountant.

"You must be Roy," the beast said with a guttural tone.

"Y—yes," Roy said. "It's, um, a privilege to meet you, Mr. Gamon."

"Gamon is fine."

"Yes sir."

"Not sir, just Gamon."

"Yes si—Gamon."

Gamon chuckled. "It's okay, friend. Relax."

Strangely enough, Roy did relax. The command alone from such a lofty mogul was enough to soothe the nerves. He stood in the presence of the mighty Gamon, victorious in his effort to rewrite the playbook, at least for a day. Roy took a measured breath and nodded.

Gamon gestured to a chair in front of the desk. "Have a seat."

Roy stepped forward and complied. He took a moment to admire the chair's sturdiness, a far cry from the rickety stools back in the sub-core. Roy glanced around a small den with very little decor, temporary in every sense of the word. An overhead light with a pull string served as the sole source of illumination.

A tense silence gripped the space as Gamon scrutinized the visitor through a narrowed gaze. He exhaled a puff of smoke through his gaping nostrils and shifted the cigar to the other side of his mouth. "So you're a plumber," he said with a snide tone.

Roy adjusted his posture. "Yes. Been working the station for over a decade."

"Tell me, then. How would you replace a busted T-line with high saline content?"

"Steel connector with greased-up niners."

The reptilian huffed. "*Niners*? Are you serious? Why in the hell would you not use—"

"A grump link?" Roy glared at the minion.

"Y—yeah."

"Because the threads are pre-coated and tend to corrode, especially when moving acidic content. Sure, they'll last a good long while, but niners are die-cast and last forever. Grump links are pretty and easy to install, but I prefer reliability over aesthetics."

Gamon glanced back at the minion and smirked.

The minion sneered in response.

Roy allowed himself a brief grin before Gamon returned his attention.

"So enlighten me, mister plumber. Why are you here?"

Roy scrunched his brow. "Huh?"

"Did I stutter?"

"Um, I sent you a message."

"I'm aware. But *why* did you send it?"

"I, um ..." Roy trailed off and glanced away.

"It's not a trick question, friend. You are aware of my trade, yes?"

Roy hesitated before responding. "You're a trafficker."

"Of what?"

"Of ..." Roy thought for a moment. "Of nothing."

Gamon nodded. "Good. So again, why are you—"

"Because my life is a worthless grind and I don't want it anymore."

Gamon grinned and leaned back in his chair.

"I'm halfway through this failure of existence and I have nothing to point at. Everything I do benefits someone else. I don't care about fame or fortune, or any other status-laden bullshit. All I want is to participate in something with real consequence. Actual repercussion, not just some empty thrill. I have skills. Applicable skills. I'm a first-class architect and a kick-ass engineer." Roy huffed and shrugged. "So why the fuck am I cleaning other people's shit?"

Gamon rapped his fingers on the desk, filling the room with dull taps of contemplation. He glanced over his shoulder to the reptilian minion, who flicked his tongue in response. The cigar shifted as he studied Roy with mysterious intent. He offered a slight nod, then folded his hands on the desktop. "Mister plumber, I need you to unclog a toilet for me."

A painful silence gripped the room.

The minion smirked.

Roy cocked his jaw, then closed his eyes to scream internally. His dignity swirled around the virtual drain and disappeared. He slapped the armrests and started to rise, initiating the long trek back to the shithole from which he came.

Gamon raised a palm, halting Roy's ascent. "Perhaps you didn't hear me, friend. I need you to unclog a toilet ... on the Sunken Isles."

The reveal sucker-punched Roy like a slighted ex-girlfriend. An eyelid twitched as his jaw slacked open. His gobsmacked brain abandoned his forearms, dropping him back into the chair with an awkward plunk.

Gamon grinned. "Do we have an understanding?"

Roy fainted and tumbled to the floor.

* * *

It should come as no surprise that the meeting between Gamon and Roy was not recorded. Gamon was too smart to allow something that stupid. This all comes from a firsthand account, namely the minion over his shoulder, a hatchet man by the name of Zip.

Do not let the cutesy name fool you, Zip earned his nickname through a ruthless efficiency, especially when it came to murder. Zip was an assassin's assassin, someone called into the fray when zealots overplayed their cards. As his many fans put it, he offered "clean whacks to dirty hacks," an event often referred to as "getting zipped."

I should reiterate that Durangoni Security is a force to be reckoned with. They snuff out the vast majority of criminal elements. However, the most clever and nefarious crooks know how to work the system from within. *That* was the pool Zip played in. In fact, Durangoni largely ignored his exploits, regarding him more as an unpaid contractor.

I say that he *was* an assassin because my interviews with Zip came by way of correctional visitation. He now lives as a captive inside the Durangoni prison system where he is serving a two-year sentence for vandalism. Ironic, by definition. Without going into too much detail, let's just say that he got some blood where it didn't belong. The guards know exactly who he is and what he does. He even speaks freely about his unsettling deeds, which are simply dismissed as fanciful fictions. Just some bloke waxing poetic ... about murder.

Much to my surprise, I liked Zip from the very beginning. Our frequent chats revealed an honest and receptive person, considerate even. He paints a worldview that is unemotional and pragmatic, which allows him to do what he does without any sort of undue attachment. In the end, the only thing he covets is a job well done.

Unlike Roy, I actually grew to respect the reptilian reaper known as Zip. Roy had always treated him like rubbish and used him as a convenient punching bag. The fact that Roy retained his head (presumably) is nothing short of a miracle. I can only chalk it up to Zip's dispassionate need to complete his tasks in a clean and timely manner.

I learned a great deal about Roy through the frank and candid lens of Zip. In fact, I would argue with clarity that Zip provided the clearest insights into Roy's perplexing character. Below is an excerpt from one of our many conversations.

I am starting to get the impression that Roy was an unpleasant person.

Roy was a dick. (hard pause)

Well, okay then.

But, considering his lot in life at the time, I would probably be a dick too. He was mad at the universe and everything in it, so it's understandable in a way. He was also very good at what he did, so I never held it against him.

Did he know about your, um, activities?

No, and it was better that way. Roy talked a lot of smack, but he never struck me as someone with an iron stomach. Gamon saw him as a blind but useful gopher. His expertise opened doors that would have otherwise required infiltration.

Speaking of Gamon, how did you two end up working together?

We met through a mutual need. Gamon runs one of the biggest distribution networks on the station, an up-and-up outfit that I greatly respect. He's one of the best getters in the game, so our paths would naturally cross at one point or another.

To make a long story short, he got conned by one of my marks, some headstrong thug with a penchant for backstabbing. Gamon offered a squeeze job and I took it. We split the return after I split the mark in half. We've been working together ever since.

(A ping interrupts the chat, followed by a guard's voice. "Good one, Zippy. You and your stories." The guard laughs nervously, then goes silent. Zip grins.)

You should have seen it. The halves peeled apart like a cheese sandwich and slapped the floor like sacks of wet blankets. The chainsaw was so wrecked, I had to throw it away.

(Ping. "Ha! Such a vivid imagination, this guy." Silence.)

In fact, I left it there in the bloody muck and winked at the nearest camera. I'm sure the footage is out there somewhere if you want to do some digging.

(Ping. "La la la, not listening. La la la." Silence.)

* * *

DISCLAIMER: The Durangoni Office of Corrections does not condone or corroborate the actions described in this work of fiction. Randal P. Throatslitter (a.k.a. "Zip") is serving an appropriate sentence for involuntary vandalism. He is an otherwise upstanding citizen of the Durangoni Space Station and no evidence of additional wrongdoing has ever been verified by our department. For reasons still unknown, he is often the target of elaborate pranks aimed at tarnishing his respectable image. We cannot stress enough that his depictions in this book are exaggerated for dramatic effect.

CHAPTER 8

There's annoyingly opulent, there's overly extravagant, there's stupidly ostentatious, there's jaw-droppingly exhibitionistic, and then there's the Sunken Isles. The simple act of explaining this locale requires some expositional flair, so I must apologize in advance. However, building the appropriate image is critical to understanding why Roy fainted in Gamon's office.

To set this stage, let's take a giant step back and define what the Durangoni Space Station actually is. This gargantuan structure endures as one of the biggest construction projects in the history of the universe. It took centuries to plan and a millennia to build. It contains more steel than the next thousand systems combined. It orbits a star as an artificial planet because it carries enough gravitational force to rip itself apart. It's large enough to have its own atmosphere and seasons, all of which require careful planning. There are beings living aboard the station right now who earn a decent living forecasting the artificial weather of an artificial world.

Durangoni houses a trillion active residents who populate the station from surface to core. It is not uncommon for beings, workers especially, to live out their entire lives inside the structure without ever setting foot (or tentacle) on the surface. As with most indulgent safaris, a trek to the surface is often regarded as too expensive. It's much easier, and arguably more enjoyable, to visit the nearest sensory deprivation service.

The surface is a realm of riches, and the Sunken Isles take it to an absurd new level.

Dissatisfied with *just* being on the surface, a wealthy pioneer decided to create a *new* surface *below* the surface. How? By enclosing a floating island inside a transparent dome and sinking it beneath an artificial ocean.

I know, right?

Grab a drink and strap in.

Floating islands are a common sight along the Rich Rings. Their surfaces are loaded with luxury resorts, sandy beaches, and numerous harbors for expensive yachts. An artificial ocean stretches around the entire structure, made possible by a miles-deep trench. The walls and base are fortified with aluminum, often a hundred meters thick at the highest pressure points. The combination of strength and lightness puts minimal strain on the station. Apart from the core itself, nothing was planned more meticulously than the ocean rings. After all, a single breach would result in a catastrophic loss of life. A solid decade of stress tests and bomb trials were performed before a single drop of water was poured.

Filling the trenches was its own titanic hurdle. A single ocean ring contains 500 quintillion gallons of water. This far outstripped the local system, so a fleet of ice harvesters was deployed to nearby comets. They dismantled entire worlds and hauled mountains of ice back to the station. The mega-payloads were deposited into the trenches where armies of robots chipped them into meltable chunks. Rocks were pulverized into sediment, allowing treatment plants to filter and repurpose it as sand for beaches.

The massive rings are wide enough to create a horizon, so standing to either side creates the image of a vast and expansive ocean. Filtration systems run around the clock, keeping the water crystal clear and pathogen-free. Their primary purpose is to act as giant aquifers. The immense pressure supplies fresh water to the entire station, rendering circulation pumps all but useless. In fact, the only pump system inside Durangoni does nothing but carry water from core basins back to surface treatment.

Station designers foresaw the appeal of ocean rings, and thus marketed their access to the uber-wealthy. Floating islands were constructed and sold to the highest bidders, often the richest beings in the universe. The custom isles were several miles in diameter and featured an array of trimmings, from palm trees and sandy beaches to volcanic rock and exotic flora. Owners were free to build on them as desired, so long as they continued to pay the ocean access fee, a sum that infused the station with a reliable (and substantial) income. The designers had created a veritable gold mine, but even they did not foresee the advent of the Sunken Isles.

Ocean access fees did exactly what they were designed to do, in that they gave island owners access to the ocean. The only problem was, the agreements never clarified what "ocean" meant, i.e. just the surface. Owners were free to use personal submarines, but nothing explicitly forbade them from turning the entire island into a submarine.

And that's exactly what Mimi Moxarion did.

Mimox, as she was known, decided that owning a floating island on a colossal space station was not exclusive enough. She, like every other island owner, was awash in affluence. Wealth at that level transcends the material world to become a competition in and of itself. It's not enough to raise a virtue flag that only a handful of beings can raise. Your flag needs to be the *only* flag.

And so, she sank her island.

Not in the traditional sense, of course. She hired a superstar team of engineers to tackle the problem, which took several years to solve. But solve it they did, and many island owners were justifiably concerned when a giant glass dome consumed their neighbor and plunged it into the ocean depths.

Mimox had raised her flag.

But it didn't last long.

Excessive wealth tends to short-sight its owners. Mimox had assumed that her neighbors would bow to her grandeur while stewing in surface jealousy. They did no such thing, because she failed to recognize a crucial piece of the equation. Her neighbors may have been filthy rich, but her superstar team of engineers was decidedly *not*. And so, they packaged the dome plans and sold them to her neighbors.

Mimox's reign ended as quickly as it began. Before long, numerous islands sank into the great blue yonder, creating a network of subterranean tropics. The Sunken Isles was born, and remains one of the most exclusive communities in the known universe.

Even so, Mimox decided to sell her island and purchase her own star. Her never-ending quest for ultimate exclusivity came to a fiery end when she constructed a lavish station home in lower orbit, the first and only "sundo" (sun-condo). The views were spectacular, but her wealth proved useless against a coronal mass ejection.

* * *

Roy and Zip strolled down a sleek corridor with no one else in sight. The white walls and seamless panels gave Roy a sense of purpose, as if tromping towards a research ship bound for adventure. And in that sense, he wasn't far off. Zip, on the other hand, maintained a forward stare as his swanky shoes clacked along the floor. His classy garb stood in stark contrast to Roy's workman duds. To the average passerby, one might assume that Zip had caught a pickpocket. But in that particular sector, the very notion of a passerby was a laughable concept.

Near the end of the tunnel, an oval portal came into view. It clung to the wall as the sole feature inside a spacious white foyer. A pair of glass doors split the port in half, leading into a dark tunnel with no markings. It would seem that anyone standing inside that particular room knew exactly where they were and where they were going.

Anyone except for Roy, of course.

Zip strolled to a stop at the center of the foyer, placing him several meters away from the portal. He crossed his arms behind his back and stared at the glass doors. Roy settled beside him and released a muted sigh. Not from annoyance, just happy to rest. Zip had slapped him awake after fainting in Gamon's office. "Follow me and mind your lip" was the command, which Roy heeded while nursing a throbbing headache. The journey up to that point had been a convoluted maze of back channels and ghost pods. The mental fog had started to clear, but Roy had no idea where he was. His gaze bounced between Zip and the portal doors.

"So—"

"Shut the fuck up," Zip said without making eye contact.

Roy swallowed a snarky retort and huffed instead.

Moments later, the dull hum of an approaching pod broke the silence. The stark tunnel slowly filled with light, signaling the arrival of a transport vessel. As it crept into view behind the doors, Roy could tell that it wasn't a normal pod. It was longer, sleeker, and a tad more ostentatious. In other words, it was a private vessel.

The doors slid open, revealing a robed male with tawny skin and prominent jade eyes. He floated into the room with strips of red fabric dangling from his folded arms. Green and gold accents gave him a kingly vibe, or at the very least, an assumption of status. An intricate head wrap matched the robe in weight and color. Roy did not recognize the species, but based on its stout frame and menacing build, it was not one to be trifled with. The creature glided to a stop between the portal and the two visitors.

"Hello, Zip," he said in a pleasant baritone.

Zip nodded. "Good to see you, Werner."

"This the plumber?"

"Seems to be."

Werner grunted, then turned to Roy. "You a plumber?"

"Last time I checked," Roy said.

Werner narrowed his gaze. "Given a flarkian framework with two gromples, three saromarko switches, and a pavrav gauge, how would you reverse a pressure spike of 200 wronks?"

Roy cocked an eyebrow and glanced at Zip.

Zip replied with a nonverbal *Answer the goddamn question.*

Roy returned his gaze to Werner, then shrugged. "Well, given that I was about to die, I would probably rub one out."

"Pardon?"

"You know, flog the cap'n. Spurt the sprite. Visit the knuckle circus."

"Um ..."

"Any pipe jockey worth their salt knows that two gromples on the same line with a pavrav gauge is a recipe for disaster. That's why half of the surrounding quadrants have outlawed the practice. You could, in theory, use a pavrav plus, but that only reduces the knock-fail from 80 to 60. And 200 wronks with *three* saromarkos? That would give you less than two minutes before a catastrophic decoupling, hardly enough time to reverse a damn thing. So again, I would probably rub one out and hope to finish before the end."

Werner eyed Zip, who rolled his eyes.

"What I *think* you are trying to ask," Roy said with a cocksure tone, "is how would I reverse a pressure spike with three saromarko *platinum* switches, a very important distinction. They are designed to negate the swells of outdated regulator tech like gromples. In which case, I would cut power to the first saromarko and spin the pavrav down to 50%. The overall pressure would drop by 25% and stabilize on its own while the other two saromarkos cancel out the gromples. And then I would *still* rub one out all over the console just to stick it to the fuck nugget who botched the configuration."

An awkward silence settled between them.

Werner nodded slowly, then turned to Zip. "I like 'em."

"That makes one of us."

Werner chuckled into a sigh. "Does he know?" he said, basically asking *Does this little twerp know that you are a ruthless murder machine that would happily gut him like a fish and wear his spleen as a hat?*

Zip sneered and shook his head.

"Know what?" Roy said, trading his gaze between the two.

"Forget about it," Werner said, then motioned for the pair to join him in the vessel. "This way, mister plumber."

* * *

Perhaps the most memorable moment from my interviews with Zip came by way of a peripheral encounter. I had asked about the events leading up to the meeting with Werner (an immensely powerful individual who we will examine shortly). Zip pondered the question for a time, as if to choose his words carefully. What I assumed was leery contemplation was anything but. He just wanted to show me the breadth of his reputation.

Zip plucked a cigarette from his pocket and tucked it between his lips, for no other reason than he could. Smoking was banned throughout the station, doubly so in prison, and triply so during visitation. Zip wasn't even a smoker, come to find out. But amazingly, a nearby guard hurried over and promptly lit the cigarette. Zip took two puffs, then snuffed it out in the guard's open palm, all while maintaining eye contact with me. The guard swallowed a whimper, then hurried back to his post and struggled to ignore the pain.

To say I was rattled would be an understatement. For the first time along the journey, the depths began to test my mettle.

Um ...

What was the question again?

That was ... something.

(Ping. "The guard was upholding the station's strict no-smoking policy by extinguishing and removing the contraband.")

(I lift my gaze to the overhead speaker.) With his own flesh?

(Ping. "Standard procedure.")

(My widened eyes return to Zip.)

(smirks) Shall we continue?

Yes, um ...

(I glance around the enclosure, feeling somewhat shaken. Zip tunes into this fact and seems to enjoy the squirming. With my dignity waning, I can do nothing but stiffen my posture and reclaim an air of confidence. And so I do. Or at least I try.)

So, um, Gamon was in cahoots with Werner Xizon Pyrak? *The* Werner Xizon Pyrak?

Everyone is in cahoots with Werner in one way or another. Given the nature of his empire, it's hard not to be. (leans forward) Where do you think your Ruutzo coffee comes from?

(Ping. "Ruutzo coffee is an illegal import and subject to customs inquiry. Should you be caught with this contraband, you will be arrested and prosecuted to the fullest extent of Durangoni law. The minimum sentence is six months in a correctional facility and a fine of 10,000 credits. An enforcement team has been deployed to 623 Bartonian Row, R312, section B4.")

623 Bart—that's my apartment!

(Ping. "Should they find any Ruutzo coffee, you will be immediately detained.")

(Zip responds with a casual wave, as if to reject pepper on his salad.)

(Ping. "I mean ... nevermind.")

(My gaze jumps between the injured guard, the overhead com, and a disturbingly calm Zip.) Um ...

Is that your favorite word?

Um ...

Exactly.

So ...

Um.

(The teasing actually resets the mood, much to my surprise. I crack a smile, despite witnessing the shocking influence of a feared assassin in real-time.)

So how long had Gamon been working with Werner?

(shrugs) Not for me to know.

I only ask from a standpoint of disparity. It seems odd to me that Gamon would let a greenhorn like Roy anywhere near someone like Werner.

You and me both. But at the same time, this was a perfect storm scenario. Werner was in desperate need of assistance, and Gamon was in desperate need to provide that assistance. Anyone below the fold knows that when Werner asks, you deliver.

Or else ...

Or else they call me.

But you were there already.

Which concerned me a bit. You see, for someone like Werner to press someone like Gamon, there had to be something critical on the line.

Like what?

(Zip leans back and crosses his arms. This time, in leery contemplation.)

* * *

As a necessary disclaimer, Puki Horpocket has never and would never consume Ruutzo coffee, despite its delicious and uniquely robust character.

While it remains an illegal substance inside Durangoni, its chemical profile is no different than any other variety. Ruutzo beans contain prototypical amounts of acids and alkaloids. The ban is entirely political in nature.

Ruutzo is a rich volcanic region of Neaz, a lush moon that orbits a desolate planet in the Abell cluster. Its parent system is largely devoid of life, except for Neaz and a hearty form of methane plankton. The Neazan people remained independent for eons, but decided to join the Federation in hopes of expanding their economic reach. Their impact was quick and fruitful, thanks in large part to their delicious produce.

However, the honeymoon period would not last long. Neazans are known for many things, but tact is not one of them. Their ruler at the time, a narcissistic chap with thin skin, insulted the quadrant ruler at the time, also a narcissistic chap with thin skin. They exchanged verbal blows, resulting in a silly battle of wits that ended with a trade embargo.

But as with most prohibitions, it had precisely the opposite effect.

The demand for Neazan goods shot through the roof, creating a thriving tourist economy that generated far more wealth than trade. The moon transformed into a luxury retreat that welcomed deep pockets from every corner of the cosmos.

When the quadrant ruler realized the mistake (read: panicked over the enormous loss of revenue), he offered to lift the embargo, but refused to apologize. The Neazan ruler famously responded with a single word: "Melamook." (Neazi is a complex language that is difficult to translate on a good day. The closest Earth reading would be "Nah, fuck you.")

The embargo has remained in place ever since.

CHAPTER 9

Roy and Zip strolled through the portal and into the sleek vessel. Werner followed them inside and the doors closed behind him. Roy's widened eyes combed the interior of an oval pod without a single sharp corner. A long bench with plush yellow padding encircled the cabin. The upper half was crafted from transparent composite, offering sweeping views of the dank tunnel interior. Obviously not the intended vista, which prodded Roy with nervous anticipation. Grip rails extended from a central hub, like the posh version of a rickety carnival ride. The vessel, it would seem, was designed for speed as well as comfort.

Roy stepped around the hub and settled onto the bench directly across from the doors. Zip and Werner sat near the front, not that the vessel had a front, given its symmetrical build. The front, in this case, was the area pointing down the tunnel. The opposite side faced a solid wall, which clued Roy into a key realization. The port was less of a train stop and more of a launch chute. His eyes traced a dim row of tunnel lights down to a blue barrier in the distance. Instinct compelled him to search for a seat belt, but Werner and Zip had relaxed into their seats without much care for safety. *When in Qwarp*, he thought, then leaned back and draped his arms across the rear cushions.

*   *   *

Qwarp is widely considered the galactic equivalent of Rome. Its rise and fall were largely similar, just on a cosmic scale. It even had a charismatic leader who got murdered by his best friend. But instead of a tragic "Et tu, Brute?" end to his reign, he mooned his comrades and shouted profanities before perishing mid-rant. History books have largely ignored that part.

*   *   *

"Initiation complete," said a pleasant feminine voice.

"Alpha Tower," Werner said.

A ping responded, followed by a soft hum of initiation.

The vessel began a slow creep through the tunnel. Roy leaned forward out of habit, but the sensation of motion was almost imperceptible. Tunnel lights whipped overhead as it gathered speed towards the blue barrier. Werner and Zip remained unfazed. They exchanged some casual banter, forcing Roy's headspace to waffle between *everything's fine* and *we're all gonna die*. As the barrier approached, it finally dawned on him. It wasn't a barrier at all. It was a pressure gate leading into the ocean.

The vessel punched through the gate and into the blue abyss. The transition was seamless, like a drop of water joining the whole. Roy watched the gate fade behind them before lifting his astounded gaze to the sea. The surface shimmered far above, but something else had dropped his jaw. A massive braid of cables lifted from the depths and clutched a suspended platform several miles across. It floated in the void, encased by a towering dome of glass.

There it was.

An actual Sunken Isle.

The braid anchored the platform to the ocean floor, where it tapped into various service lines. Titanium tethers prevented the domes from crashing into one another. Countless conduits snaked around the tethers, feeding the isles with power, plumbing, and a host of other needs. Roy rose to his feet and twisted around the enclosure with mouth agape. A multitude of domes and braids floated in the deep like a school of monstrous jellyfish. Never in his wildest dreams could he have concocted such a vision.

"First time here?" Werner said.

Roy collapsed back into his seat, heeding a pair of weakened knees. His eyes continued to scan the glorious vista above. "First time anywhere. I live near the core and my work keeps me there. When I do break away, it ain't to a place like this."

Werner smirked.

"So ..." Roy's gaze wandered over to Werner. "You need a plumber?"

"Yes," Werner said with a matter-of-fact tone.

Roy responded with a blank stare, clearly expecting some details, but derailed by receiving bupkis. His eyes shifted as he searched for a reasonable follow-up question. None of them were as relevant as the first, so he kept staring like a stoned hippie.

Werner sighed and glared at Zip. "Did Gamon not give him the rundown?"

Zip shrugged and deflected the glare to Roy.

"What's your understanding of the situation?" Werner said to Roy.

"All I heard was 'plumber' and 'Sunken Isles' before I passed out."

Werner groaned and shook his head. After a brief ponder (and another glare at Zip), he crossed his arms and locked eyes with Roy. "Are you familiar with Subatomic Transport?"

Roy snorted-chuckled. "You mean Shrink Ray Shipping?"

Werner narrowed his gaze. "It's a little more complicated than that."

"And illegal as hell. You remember that whole, um ... y'know."

Werner narrowed his gaze further.

"But yes, I'm familiar with it. At least, as much as a peasant can be. Something about sucking atoms dry."

"Well, that's a grossly uneducated way to put it."

Roy sneered in response.

"Atoms are mostly empty space. The physical matter consisting of the nucleus and electrons only occupy a tiny fraction of the whole. The concept behind Subatomic Transport is to remove that space for ease of shipping."

"Like a shrink ray," Roy said with a smarmy grin.

* * *

"Shrink Ray Shipping" was a highly offensive nickname in the industry, of which Werner was the top dog. The methodology received widespread mockery when a giant dildo untethered from its gravity-bind and re-expanded inside a space station, destroying the structure and killing everyone inside. When images emerged of a massive pink cock inside a giant debris cloud, one reporter said, "Well that station got proper-fucked." The clip went viral and Subatomic Transport was swiftly outlawed, deemed far too dangerous for commercial use. "Shrink Ray Shipping," as the media dubbed it, was relegated to powerful sects of organized crime.

* * *

Werner huffed and glared at Zip (again) while reconsidering the arrangement.

Zip sighed and rolled his eyes while reconsidering a double murder.

After some more-than-obvious social cues, Roy sensed the contempt and could feel his appeal slipping away. "Sorry," he said with a sheepish tone. "Bad joke."

"Anyway," Werner said, "my distribution network still uses this tech in a ... somewhat flexible capacity. Do you understand?"

Roy nodded.

"We move great quantities of goods between buyers and sellers.

Simple as that."

"Okay. So why do you need a plumber?"

"Sometimes a shipment gets contaminated. When a corrupted unit expands, it activates the whole and sparks a catastrophic inflation. We can normally deal with this at an extraction facility, but certain cargo types require a little more discretion."

"You didn't answer my question."

Werner smirked, then reached into his breast pocket and withdrew a puck of material. He tossed it at Roy, who caught it with an awkward fumble.

Roy opened his palm and inspected the mysterious puck. It was a few inches wide and forged from a glassy resin. Smooth to the touch, but very hard and heavy. The puck was lighter than an ingot, but dense enough to be dangerous. Roy could tell right away that its rounded edges were more for safety than aesthetics. A clump of dark matter rested in the center, which consumed a third of the overall volume.

"What is this?" Roy said.

"42 billion vials of medication."

"*Billion?*" Roy eyed Werner in disbelief. "How is that possible?"

"Mass retained, space removed. Atoms locked in stasis."

"But it's so light. How do you account for weight?"

"And *that*, mister plumber, is why I'm a very rich man."

Roy grunted, then bounced the puck in his hand. "So what's the drug?"

"Snake Bone."

Roy yelped and dropped the puck, which clanked on the floor and wobbled to a rest.

Werner grinned.

* * *

Roy's fearful reaction was far from unwarranted. Snake Bone is a highly addictive, highly dangerous, and highly illegal drug. It has a complex chemical makeup and a lengthy technical name that willfully neglects vowels. "Snake Bone" is the go-to slang, which was earned during another viral news clip.

A pair of field reporters was filming an info-series about the effects of illegal drugs. One would stay sober and serve as the interviewer. The other would trip on various drugs and serve as the interviewee. It was promoted as a scared-straight campaign, which enjoyed notable success. Some episodes were funnier than intended, but still applauded. Others were steeped in horror and deemed highly effective.

And then there was the Snake Bone episode, the most infamous of the bunch.

The drug was notorious for its strong hallucinogenic effects. It occupied a strange realm in the drug trade because it carried no biological threat. It was largely benign, no more dangerous than a weak cup of coffee. However, the psychedelic effects were second to none. The drug sent the user into a kaleidoscopic dreamscape (or nightmare) that lasted for days.

And therein lay the danger.

The prolonged exposure resulted in countless deaths. There was no such thing as "bring a friend and enjoy the ride." A user could start tripping on their own couch, then wake up a week later in the next quadrant, naked, bloody, and in desperate need of a lawyer.

The drug was developed as a psych med, which worked a little too well. The problem was, the powerful trip was often stronger than the patient's incapacity, rendering them as lethargic as a Goth teen. As they say, when you stare into the void of truth, there's nowhere left to go.

Snake Bone eventually slithered into the public sphere, which created an immediate and voracious demand. The resulting black market basically ran itself. It can be a highly profitable venture for anyone willing to shoulder the risk. Durangoni houses a powerful security force with very little oversight, so the risk can be substantial. "Bone Brokers," as dealers are known, often disappear without a trace.

But anyway, back to the episode.

One reporter took a dose while the other sat and waited. He didn't wait long, because things got weird in a hurry. The imbiber gawked at his own limbs, which had developed minds of their own. The sober reporter commenced the now-infamous short-lived interview. While staring into the great beyond, the drugged reporter uttered the most memorable line of his career: "My bones are snakes, and that's the least of it." The poor fool was carried to the hospital, where he tripped in a padded room for several days.

From that day forward, the drug was forever known as "Snake Bone."

* * *

Roy had scurried to the opposite end of the vessel. He stood atop the bench with his back to the wall, pointing a shaking finger at the puck. "What in Tim's Blue Hell are you doing with 42 billion doses of Snake Bone?!"

"I figured that would be obvious," Werner said.

"That's some wicked fucking voodoo right there!"

Zip pursed his lips and nodded in agreement.

"Oh for fuck's sake." Werner rose from his seat and moseyed over to the puck. He scooped it off the floor and banged it against a grip rail. Sharp clanks echoed around the cabin, causing Roy to flinch with each hit. "This thing can withstand a million plasma blasts. You're in no danger, so get your filthy feet off my leather."

The sting of ridicule pulled Roy down to the floor. He cowered like a scorned puppy and shuffled back to his original seat.

Werner grumbled as he pocketed the puck and returned to his own seat.

Zip had donned a disconcerted expression as he stared off into oblivion, reliving his own wayward adventures with slithering bones.

Moments later, the vessel breached the surface, sending ribbons of water down the hull and showering the cabin with sunlight. However, this was not the actual surface, nor the actual sun. The vessel had breached the atmospheric bubble created by Werner's Sunken

Isle dome. They were now inside a private tropical paradise, complete with sandy shores, lapping waves, and an artificial weather system.

The shuttle hovered above the surface as it pushed towards the nearest shoreline. A mile of water rested between the dome and the island, creating a liquid donut of sorts. The island itself was held at the center by a strong magnetic field. Roy could see dunes and palm trees along the shore as the vessel approached, but strangely enough, no structures. The plot was barren, like a ghostly desert in the middle of nowhere. He stood for a better view, but uncovered nothing. The platform lingered as little more than a blank canvas.

"Well that's disappointing," Roy said.

Werner cocked an eyebrow. "What, an entire island suspended beneath the ocean is not good enough for you?"

"No, I mean, I thought these were supposed to be like, luxury resorts or something."

"This isn't that kind of island."

Moments later, the shuttle transitioned from water to land, churning a cloud of sand in its wake. It floated up the first dune, zipping by palm trees and grassy mounds. Roy watched with cautious interest as the vessel crested the sandy hill. The beach disappeared, snapped away by a sudden transition. The rim of a giant metal valley passed below the vessel, initiating its descent towards the center. The bowl stretched for several miles in every direction, consuming the vast majority of real estate. Its white sheen created the image of a massive satellite dish, primed and ready to receive its digital bounty.

But it wasn't that kind of dish.

The vessel slowed as it approached the center of the dish. Roy glanced around the interior, now awash in reflective light. The rim towered over them like a peakless mountain. A sense of intrusion filled Roy with unease. This was a guarded place, a deep chasm that few knew existed. A place, he presumed, that he could lose his life for seeing.

Werner studied the plumber's reaction without saying a word.

Zip maintained his disinterest. Either he'd seen it before or didn't care in the slightest.

The shuttle pinged, then slowed to a stop and lowered to the ground. The doors slid open, prompting Werner to rise and mosey towards the exit. A gust of tropical air swirled around the cabin. Roy inhaled the briny sweetness, which jostled some distant memories. He could see his homeworld. Bronze beaches, copper sunsets, the same salty air. His cheeks puckered as a smile crept across his face. An actual smile, conjured by a long-neglected muscle memory. And then his ex-wife leaned into the mental frame and killed it all.

"Goddamnit," Roy said. "She even got my memories in the divorce."

"Come again?" Werner said from outside the shuttle.

"Nothing." Roy sighed, then noticed the puck in Werner's hand.

Werner grunted with dismissal, then retrieved a docking device from his pocket. A pair of rounded claws protruded from the handheld base, like a comdev with a handcuff attached. Roy squinted with curiosity as Werner affixed the puck and entered an activation code. The device pinged and a mounting rod rose from the dish. It stopped at chest-height, allowing Werner to connect the device. A drop and twist locked it into place, creating the unsettling portrait of a hostile lollipop. Werner wiped his hands and returned to his seat inside the vessel. The doors closed and the shuttle continued its journey across the dish.

Roy watched the puck assembly fade into the distance as the shuttle climbed its way to the upper rim. He cocked his neck and turned to Werner, clearly confused by the action. Questions were mounting, but a strong apprehension kept his mouth shut.

Werner smirked at the plumber.

Roy was in the game now, and they both knew it.

* * *

Suffice to say, my conversations with Zip provided the most detail into Roy's underworld antics. And given Zip's utter indifference to his captive status, I had no reason to doubt him. It should also be noted that Werner's Sunken Isle dishworld no longer exists. The very nature of The Incident would ensure its destruction.

Roy still had no idea what was happening?

He may have had a clue, but I couldn't say for sure. In any regard, Roy had gleaned enough smarts to roll with the punches. His insolence was hard to wrangle, but even he could see that silence equaled survival.

Just so we're clear, Werner was transporting 42 *billion* doses of *Snake Bone*.

(nods) Yup.

And that didn't concern you?

(shrugs) Why would it?

Well, for starters, that's easily one of the highest capital offenses one could imagine.

You say that like Werner suffers the law.

Doesn't everyone?

(chuckles) *That*, Mr. Horpocket, is adorably naive.

(Ping. "The enforcement power of Durangoni Security is absolute. No individual, citizen or otherwise, is above the law.")

Seems like a reasonable assertion.

(smirks) Garko! Punch yourself in the face!

(The guard behind Zip sighs, then removes his helmet and wallops his own cheek.)

Again!

(Smack.)

Again!

(Smack. His nose begins to bleed.)

Thank you, Garko.

(The guard wipes the blood from his face and puts his helmet back on. Zip softens his smirk and gives me a subtle nod, as if to curtsy after murdering my calm.)

Point taken.

(Ping. "Did something happen? Our feed cut out for a moment.")

CHAPTER 10

Roy turned his attention to the approaching rim, where a lone pillar loomed over the giant basin. The structure stood several stories tall and resembled an airspace control tower, complete with an observation deck. The opaque glass gave it a menacing persona, like an evil eye standing watch over its domain.

The shuttle crested the rim and slowed to a stop beside the tower. The doors slid open with a ping of arrival. Werner and Zip stood from their seats and wandered outside without a word. Roy stayed put, partly out of fear, partly out of confusion. The decorum he knew no longer applied, so he awaited basic instructions like a nerdy kid at summer camp.

Zip moseyed towards an entry door at the base of the tower.

Werner paused and turned back to the shuttle port. "This way, mister plumber."

Roy took a deep breath, then rose to his feet and exited the shuttle. He passed through the oval port and stepped down to a concrete platform that surrounded the tower. Several palm trees lined the perimeter with green fronds rustling in the wind. Roy lifted his gaze to the bright blue sky. Or rather, the dome's projection of a bright blue sky. A handful of white clouds roamed the space, blotting the artificial sun from time to time. Roy could feel the heat on his skin, leaving him to wonder if the dome emitted radiation. *Definitely a question for another time*, he wisely thought to himself.

"Is this actual UV?" Roy said.

Werner cocked an eyebrow. *That's your most burning question?* he conveyed without saying a word. He turned towards the tower and resumed his approach.

Roy swallowed the scorn and followed.

A short trek later, the group reassembled outside the tower entrance. Zip stood in front of a drab gray door with his arms crossed. Werner paused alongside and turned to Roy, who took his final steps.

"Understand, mister plumber. What you are about to do cannot be undone. Your actions from this point on are a pledge of confidence. Should you violate that confidence, your life, as well as the lives you cherish, is forfeit."

Roy gulped. "Understood."

"Good. Then let's unclog this toilet."

Zip grabbed the handle and yanked it upwards. The door clanked like a bank vault, then swung open with a slow whine. Werner floated into the tower base, a drab receiving area that housed an elevator shaft and little else. He summoned the lift as Roy shuffled into the dim room with arms pinned to his side. The trapped air was thick with humidity, no doubt from baking in the sun all day. Zip followed him inside and latched the door shut, turning the dim sauna into a dark coffin. The elevator pinged soon after and a door slid open, revealing a cramped car that two people would find uncomfortable.

Werner stepped inside, spun around, and pressed his back to the rear wall. Roy followed him in and filled much of the remaining area, careful to avoid Werner's personal space. Zip pushed his way inside and crammed Roy into a corner, dropping any pretense of civility. He pressed the only available button and the door slid shut.

An awkward silence filled the space, broken only by the dull hum of ascent. Roy yearned for some cheesy elevator music to break the tension, but he would have to make do with the screams inside his head. Luckily the ride was short, four stories by his estimate. A ping of arrival echoed through the cabin and the door slid open. Zip exited the car, leaving Roy to peel himself off the wall and regain some dignity.

"About time you got here," said a stern feminine voice.

Roy peeked into a control center filled with chirping gauges and blinking lights. He searched for the voice, but was cut short by Werner shoving him in the back.

"Had to fetch the plumber," he said. "You know that."

Roy stumbled to a stop outside the elevator. Werner floated around him and into the control room, a rounded enclosure about ten meters wide. A small observation deck rested at the center, which Werner claimed. It loomed over a large crescent terminal with three distinct stations. The entire console faced a panoramic viewport that overlooked the basin. Various live feeds hovered above the port, everything from dome views to puck zooms.

"And where did you fetch him from? The Kink Rinks?"

Roy turned to the central station, where a chair swiveled towards Werner. An alien female with light blue skin and dark lips revealed herself. Fleshy black dreads were pulled into a ponytail, with single strands dangling above her cheeks. Her build was short and stout, but her attitude towered over the group. Large amber eyes hurled visual daggers at Werner, dismissing Roy's presence altogether.

"We've been waiting here for *hours*," she said.

Werner shrugged. "Gamon had a lead, which took a bit to snag. You know the drill, so feel free to get off my back."

She huffed and turned to Roy. "This the guy?"

"Yup," Werner said. "Sharp fella, too."

Roy allowed his gaze to wander, combing her from head to toe like a creepy pervert. A leather ensemble clung to her frame, giving her a stylish yet practical vibe. The duds looked well-lived and well-loved, a quality that instantly captivated Roy. When his eyes reached her studded boots, she snapped him to attention.

Roy flinched and met her disgusted gaze.

She whipped a finger at the adjacent station. "You're over here, fuckwit."

Roy grinned as if she had asked him out to dinner. He traced her rigid arm to the station on her left, where Zip was prepping the console. Roy sauntered over to the chair as her berating of Werner continued in the background. Zip completed his task and stepped aside, allowing Roy to assume the position. He plopped into the chair, then cracked his knuckles and fanned his fingers as if to work a pipe organ. A hologram grid of bars and gauges glowed beneath his hands, the nerve center for the island's pumps and pressure controls. Each section linked to a map of the isle, creating a handy mental image. A quick scan uncovered nothing abnormal, just standard functions on a massive scale.

"Any questions?" Zip said from over Roy's shoulder.

Roy pictured himself back at The Pipes, adjusting pressure gauges with beer in-hand and a roaring backdrop. "Nope. Piece of cake," Roy said, and actually meant it.

Zip patted his shoulder and stepped away, a rare moment of camaraderie between the two.

Roy smiled, gave the controls another once-over, then spun towards the bewitching beauty that was his console neighbor. She ignored his peripheral gaze, content to trade verbal barbs with Werner. Roy watched her flailing fists and spewing saliva through an amorous glow, but then an insectoid leaned into view from behind her. Roy flinched and kicked backwards, startled by the reveal. The creature occupied the third station, but hadn't said a word since they arrived. Its buggy eyes stared at Roy with an unsettling curiosity, like a praying mantis pining for a snack. A bronze carapace with spikes and nubs rendered clothing unnecessary. Without warning, it lifted a plated hand with needle-like fingers and ... waved politely.

Roy returned the wave after a horrified pause.

The insectoid nodded and went back to its own business.

The background commotion returned to Roy's ears.

"That's quite enough, Vierra," Werner said in retort.

A sudden rush of butterflies invaded Roy's stomach. His gaze jerked over to Zip, who was leaning against the wall next to the elevator shaft. Zip cocked his brow and nodded, as if to say, "Yes, *that*

Vierra."

Vierra Belliosa was a living legend inside Durangoni, a superstar engineer who designed several of the core's modern components. As the story goes, she grew weary of her rock star-like fame and decided to abandon her post. She offloaded most of her wealth and disappeared into the station to work on projects that sparked her interest, everything from perpetual motion machines to helping random kids with their science projects (under a pseudonym of course). However, her core systems were so complex that only she knew how to maintain them. Realizing this, she left a summoning program behind, the Durangoni equivalent of the Bat-Signal. Whenever a critical problem arose, the engineering team launched the signal, prompting her to log into the servers and fix it remotely. She became a literal ghost in the machine.

"Don't you dare patronize me, you wormy little shit," Vierra said to Werner.

Werner signed. "Okay, okay, calm d—"

Vierra cocked her chin and pierced him with a nonverbal *Say it and I'll eat your soul.*

Werner swallowed his words and recoiled, opting to change the subject as quickly as possible. "Alright then, shall we get this show on the road?"

Vierra narrowed her gaze, lobbing a final *fuck you* before spinning back to her station.

Zip slurped a mug of coffee in the background, which diffused the tension a bit. There was something about a well-dressed reptilian enjoying some hot java that felt supremely out of place in the current predicament. Even Werner turned to look, which seemed to reset the entire stage. Zip was surprised by the sudden attention, which he responded to by taking another wet slurp. Werner sighed, then spun to regain control of the room.

"Okay, listen up," he said with a clap.

Roy swiveled to face him.

Vierra ignored him, but kept an open ear.

The insectoid spun to face him, crossing two of its six limbs.

"We have a corrupted puck that needs cleansing. Same dealio, different locale. But for the sake of the new guy and the ... let's say, *problematic* nature of the contents, I'm going to lay this out crystal clear. Capiche?"

They all nodded, albeit in different directions.

"Each of you controls a critical aspect of the island."

Werner pointed at Roy. "Plumbing."

He pointed at the back of Vierra's head. "Systems."

He pointed at the insectoid. "Electrical."

The insectoid chirped in response, which the console automatically translated. "Tight," it said in a metallic voice.

"You're a gem, Orick," Werner said, then turned his attention to the giant dish outside the viewport. "What we have here are 42 billion units of pharma, each housed in their own titan orb container." (Read: super strong, yet oddly light baseball.) "We are going to expand ten million units at a time, all of which will drop into the basin and roll to the reservoir for processing." He tapped an icon on his own control panel. The base around the puck mount detached in sections and lowered from view, exposing a large drop zone beneath the dish. "With me so far?" he said to the group, but eyed Roy.

Roy nodded.

Vierra grunted.

Orick chirped. "Locked and cocked," the console said.

"Each expansion will take a few minutes to process. Ten million into 42 billion is a lot of time sitting on your asses, so get comfortable."

Vierra sighed.

"When the corrupted unit expands, it will cause a chain reaction that expands the rest. We hope to have at least half of the units processed by that time, which will minimize stress on the isle. Please understand that atomic space is *created*, not *consumed*. Therefore, you are going to see spikes in pressure, equilibrium, etc. Your job is to manage those spikes, the worst of which will occur during the chain reaction. Do you understand?" He eyed Roy again.

"Yes sir," Roy said.

Vierra grunted.

Orick chirped. "Indeedily do," the console said.

"Good. Then prepare for the first extraction. Orick, spin up the rod."

Orick chirped. "On it, bossman," the console said as he spun to his station.

Roy heeded the cue and spun to his own station. He tweaked a few settings to get a feel for the hologram controls. Not that there was any feel, per se, but the motions were quite intuitive. The tech used finger positions and eye tracking to gauge response, which it did extremely well. Roy, after all, was used to a more tactile experience. His muscle memory was filled with grips and twists, not taps and swipes. In any regard, he took to the system like a xanpurk to plorpis. (Read: a blind duck to cold soup. An odd translation, but still technically works.)

With prep complete, his gaze lifted to the live feeds overhead. The mounting rod and puck clamp were glowing with a massive energy charge, expelling pops of blue lightning. The puck itself was pulsing with its own current. A deep purple glint flashed and retracted several times per second, giving the impression of a building climax. The entire rig hummed over the drop zone like a star swelling to supernova.

Roy held his breath.

Orick chirped. "Ready to pop pop pop," the console said.

A hush consumed the tower.

Even Zip, the avatar of detachment, craned his neck for a better view.

Werner pulled his gaze across the console, then over the live feeds, then down to the basin. He expelled a weighted sigh, then gestured to Orick. "Release."

Orick tapped a large green icon.

The puck emitted a burst of purple light and belched a hulking mass of titan orbs. They raised high into the air and spread like the petals of a glittering flower. Ten million orbs rained into the bowl like an explosion of popcorn. A sonic boom crashed into the tower, drawing an involuntary gasp from Roy. Windows rattled as the blast bounced around the isle dome. Waves of silver orbs tumbled down the gentle slope and vanished into the drop zone.

The event left Roy wholly dumbstruck. His jaw dangled as he watched the orbs from afar, like a steely ocean disappearing through a massive drain. A handful of icons blinked from green to yellow, signaling a disturbance in the force. He corrected some minor pressure tilts, restoring the island to its baseline. *Easy breezy*, he thought to himself.

"Systems?" Werner said to Vierra.

"Fine," she said like a petulant preteen.

"Electrical?"

Orick chirped. "Smooth 'n groovy," the console said.

"Plumbing?"

"All good," Roy said.

"Excellent. Orick, you have the floor."

Orick chirped. "Cool cool cool," the console said. "Round two incoming."

Another pop, rain, and roll.

Another island reset.

Werner nodded with approval, then joined Zip for a cup of coffee.

Soon after, they did it again.

Orick chirped. "Round three incoming," the console said.

At this point, one might ask, what would be the chances of the entire lot exploding on the third round? Well, that would be a simple computation: 42 billion units, divided by 10 million per round, minus two completed. That's a one in 4,198 chance.

And unfortunately, that's exactly what happened.

A flash of purple light thundered into a gigantic mushroom cloud. The blast consumed the basin and blotted out the sky, shrouding the isle in darkness. A colossal plume of orbs careened off the dome and rained across the island like a monstrous hailstorm, pelting the beaches and splashing into the ocean. The entire structure whined like a wounded whale. The ground quaked as a violent shockwave toppled trees and conjured sand tornadoes. A tidal wave of orbs crashed into the tower and washed over the rim like a raging tsunami. The control center erupted into chaos. Every feed flashed red with critical alerts. Alarms blared from the console as Werner and Zip watched helplessly from the observation platform. Vierra stood over the central station, swiping and tapping furiously while shouting commands. Orick squawked while playing whack-a-mole at his station. The console barked "Fuck! Fuck! Fuck! Shit! Fuck!" as a reasonable translation.

Roy, on the other hand, remained oddly quiet. The initial explosion had drawn a sharp yelp, but then he fell silent. He digested the problem and leaned back in his chair, having decided that the situation was properly fucked. His console flashed alerts like a red-tinted strobe light, but he didn't seem to mind. Unlike everyone else in the room, Roy had a secret superpower (minus the acidy spit). As a regular at The Pipes, he knew how to relax inside a cauldron of chaos. And so, he stood from his chair and wandered to the rear for a cup of coffee.

The Sunken Isle, on the other hand, was ready to implode.

"What the fuck are you doing?!" Vierra shouted at Roy.

Werner and Zip echoed the sentiment through gobsmacked faces.

"Fuck! Fuck! Shit!" the console continued.

Roy poured himself some coffee, then turned back to the group. He lifted the mug for a sip, but then the tower jostled. He wobbled for balance and was able to save the spill. He smiled and winked at Werner. "That was close."

Zip's dumbfounded gaze whipped between Roy and the empty chair.

Werner shouted questions at Vierra, who shouted back heated retorts.

Orick kept abusing the console translator.

Roy sipped his coffee while studying the live feeds. Data panels whizzed through alerts like hurried movie credits. After a spell of contemplation, he wandered back to his station and stood over the controls. All eyes turned to him, not that he noticed or cared. He took another sip, then tapped a master switch near the bottom of the console. With a calm and steady finger, he swiped across a long row of icons, sending power to them all.

Then it began to rain.

The dome opened all of its shower lines, dousing the island with an artificial rainstorm. Moments later, a few pressure icons blinked from critical to caution. Then they blinked from caution to nominal. The rest of the icons followed suit, slowly returning the island to baseline pressures. Systems restored. Electrical recovered. Alerts and sirens faded away. After several harrowing minutes, the entire network had stabilized. Billions of titan orbs still littered the island, but the implosion had been neutralized.

Roy took another sip while watching the rainfall. A smile puckered his cheeks as droplets pattered the cracked viewport. His gaze fell to the console, where an effects panel snagged his attention. He tapped a lightning icon, which generated some flashes and thunder. "Neat," he said, then took another swig.

He turned to the group, who had retained their wide-eyed stares at the plumber.

Vierra stuttered into a question. "Wha—what just happened?"

Roy shrugged. "Controlled pressure reversal."

Orick chirped. "Huh?" the console said.

"Well," Roy said, "the orbs displaced a shit ton of space, which pushed a lot of water beneath the dome and out into the ocean. The shorelines dropped over 50 feet, but I couldn't just re-flood the beaches. The suction alone would have swamped the island. I couldn't release the valves all at once, because, well, big fucking red flag to station security. We needed a slow re-introduction of loss, preferably from above the shoreline." He leaned onto the console and took a cocky swig. "So I made it rain."

Vierra replied with a slight grin.

Orick chirped. "Fuckin' a," the console said.

Werner stepped down from the platform and over to Roy's station. He slowed to a stop and nodded intently, as if to contemplate his fate. After a tense silence, Werner unraveled his arms and extended an open hand. "Stellar work, mister plumber."

Roy smiled and completed the shake.

* * *

Zip stared at his folded hands atop the table. It was the only time I saw him show a hint of emotion. I will never forget that moment. It felt like unearthing a glittering diamond after toiling in the darkest of mines.

Roy saved your life.

(nods) Saved us all.

And yet, you still hold him in contempt?

(shrugs and resumes his menace) An asshole savior is still an asshole. And besides, his long march to the Jackass Hall of Fame had only just begun.

CHAPTER 11

It should be noted that the Definitive Directory of Durangoni does not report on the private lives of citizens. (Unless they are rampant exhibitionists and request that we do.) Citizens are free to provide personal details, but default profiles are limited to residential addresses. What citizens do inside those residences is known only to them.

This fact rings doubly true for the Sunken Isles. Their owners remain some of the richest and most powerful beings in the universe. As such, they are largely invisible to the prying eyes of the government. In a very real sense, they *are* the government.

This is why the Snake Bone Mushroom Cloud Extravaganza cannot be confirmed. The only thing I know for certain is that Werner Xizon Pyrak had owned the isle in question and no longer does. In fact, there is no evidence to suggest that the expansion basin even existed at all. I can only rely on firsthand accounts, one of which is a murderous psychopath. That alone would be enough for any reasonable reporter to dismiss the event outright. Or at the very least, take it with a giant grain of salt.

But as with every shady tale, there's always a tiny ray of light.

In spite of all the barriers erected between me and the truth, I managed to secure another firsthand account. One that I was honestly shocked to acquire.

Vierra Belliosa.

In the time-honored tradition of full disclosure, Vierra actually reached out to yours truly. Word had reached her ear that I was writing a book on Roy. She spent a great deal of time with the green-skinned folk hero and I was initially skeptical of her intent, but she put my worries to rest shortly into the interview.

Per her invitation, we met at a beach resort on her favorite ocean ring. Below is a faithful transcript from that meeting. Readers be warned, she has a spicy persona and revels in candid language. Delicate ears may find offense.

* * *

There is something you should know about Puki Horpocket. As an esteemed editor for the most widely used periodical on the largest space station in the cosmos, the term "casual" rarely applies to my lifestyle. When I go to work, I wear a suit. When I meet a friend for drinks, I wear a suit. When it's time to shower, I take off a suit. And so, you could probably surmise what I was wearing when I strolled up to a straw hut at a luxurious beach resort. To say I looked out of place would be a gross understatement. I looked like a secret agent, minus the secret.

The sand in my dress shoes was starting to chafe, so I was relieved to park my bum on a barstool. A handful of patrons surrounded the square hut. They sipped on frilly cocktails while eye-humping each other in skimpy beach attire. I selected the corner nearest the water, which afforded me glorious views while cloaked in shade. Lounge chairs and umbrellas littered the sands, most of them occupied by superb specimens of the physical form. The exclusivity of ocean rings meant that perfect bodies abounded. Every time I visit, I always leave a little less confident in my own appeal.

Vierra must have picked up on this insecurity, because she goaded me from the minute she sat down. I didn't even see her coming. As I was gazing across the shimmering ocean waves, a blue-skinned female in an orange bikini plopped onto the barstool next to me. Her fleshy dreads were hanging free, framing her alluring amber eyes. I remember thinking that she looked alien, despite living on a colossal space station filled with a trillion aliens. Her features and proportions were slightly exaggerated, like a cartoon come to life. She oozed confidence from the get-go, despite flaunting an average build among a sea of god-like physiques. I could sense right away that she didn't have to prove a damn thing to anyone. She was a legend, and the gods were lucky to be in her presence.

Vierra Belliosa, I presume.

Whaddup, whore?

It's Horpocket. Puki Horpocket.

I didn't misspeak, jackass.

(We share a brief yet awkward silence. Vierra motions to a bartender, who promptly fills a shot of rum and sets it in front of her. She tosses it down her gullet and cluck-slides the glass back to the bartender.)

In any regard, it is both an honor and privilege to meet you.

Mhmm.

But I must admit, I am very surprised to be here at all. Zip was more amenable, given his incarceration. But you? I would have figured that anonymity was paramount.

Psh. I am the very essence of untouchable. My systems keep this bitch afloat, so an action on me is akin to suicide. They know that, I know that, and they know that I know that.

It's often said that pride goes before the fall.

(chuckles) *Pride?* I suffer many emotions, but pride isn't one of them.

That seems unlikely, given your momentous achievements.

I'm proud of my work, sure. But that's not the same as pride in stature. Think of it like this, someone can take pride in baking the world's greatest meatloaf, which is an entirely subjective ranking. I have no interest in such acclaim. I would rather invent the *oven* that bakes the world's greatest meatloaf. At that point, I control the baker's reputation. Never underestimate the desire to maintain status. People will drain their bank accounts before they part with cool points.

This coming from one of the coolest citizens in all of Durangoni.

(shrugs) Never sought it, don't care if I lose it. I can't help the fact that people think my shit is worth sniffing.

But you have created some of the most sophisticated systems that govern our world. Hell, your relay network alone has assured the purest drinking water throughout the station. If anyone has earned a bask in the spotlight, it's you.

(huffs) Bragging is for broken people. I don't give a fuck about notoriety. And besides, being awesome is like being pretty. If you have to tell people you are, then you're probably not.

So why did you reach out to me then?

Because I care about Roy. I don't want to see his name dragged through the mud.

Well, he *was* the driving force behind The Incident.

(smirks) Was he now?

You disagree?

Didn't say that. But now I'm curious to hear your take.

Fair enough. Let's start with the Sunken Isle episode. According to Zip, Werner Xizon Pyrak solicited the help of three professionals, including Roy and yourself, to cleanse a subatomic transport puck, one that was filled with illegal contraband.

That's right.

As Zip further explains, the extraction went awry and Roy single-handedly saved the island from a catastrophic implosion.

Correct. He "made it rain." (She chuckles and slaps the counter.) Still makes me laugh. You know, despite his foot-in-mouth proclivity, he did have a healthy sense of humor.

What happened to all the Snake Bone orbs?

Cleaned 'em up, I suppose. Our work was done, so we left. I imagine Werner brought in one of his reduction crews. It was a total fucking mess. The entire water rim looked like a kiddie pool stuffed with floatie toys. Probably took weeks to rectify.

Did you and Roy leave together?

No. Zip took him back to Gamon. I didn't see him again until the casino job.

Ah, the casino job, which set the stage for—

Listen, chatterbox. (She leans forward and rests on her elbows.) You may print my words so long as you print them all. Understand?

Yes.

Roy was a good guy. A talented guy. Not just some cocky prick with a few skills to rub together. Sure, he was brash and pettish, but what underappreciated artist isn't?

You make him sound like some sort of genius.

He was, in his own way. I wouldn't trust him to watch my nirfop (read: near-immortal cactus). But, he could stand side-by-side with any core engineer. It still boggles the mind that he was working as a plumber and living in the sub-core. With a little guidance, he could have been a Durangoni superstar. Make sure your readers understand that.

I will. You have my word.

(Vierra motions for two shots of rum, which the bartender promptly supplies. She pushes one over to me, which I hesitantly accept. We clink our glasses and toss them back together. Vierra clunk-slides hers back to the bartender while I cough and hack like a wuss.)

What in the bloody hell was that? Borklum battery acid?

(She chuckles and motions for two more.)

* * *

A small service pod sailed through the open space between two central rings. It was alone inside a void of nothing, whipping along an invisible tube of magnetism. The drab hull served as a stark contrast to the sleek trains passing overhead. Cargo movers were designed to blend into the background. They were the unseen drones that worked around the clock, making them ideal transports for nefarious types.

Zip and Roy sat inside, staring at each other from opposite walls. Waning sunlight peeked through small viewports, not that either of them cared. It was hard to find interest in such things after nearly perishing on a Sunken Isle. The day was effectively shot, so they sat there in silence, staring at each other, but lost inside their own heads.

The crates they sat upon were strapped to the wall, as was everything else. Cargo did not need comfort, so the ride was much bumpier than the shuttles. Sharp turns resulted in stiff arms and sore shoulders. Zip guarded a bag that squished around like a sack of gelatin. It was a large duffle with sturdy straps, one of which wrapped around his scaly hand. Zip had retrieved it from the tower base just before they departed. The constant sloshing had needled Roy's curiosity since the moment they left. He knew not to pry, so he kept his mouth shut.

"What's that?" Roy said and pointed at the bag.

The other plumber, Zip thought. "Laundry," he said after a brief pause.

"Sounds like it needed more time in the drier."

Sounds like you need a knife to the throat. "Perhaps."

Roy nodded, then resumed not saying a damn thing.

The pod punched through a vacuum barrier at the base of the next ring and began its winding approach to the shopping district. Before long, Zip and Roy found themselves strolling through the same bazaars back to Gamon's lair. Luxury surrounded them, from swanky shoppers grazing jewelry counters to the glittering chandeliers hovering along the ceiling. Roy eyed it all through a brand new lens. What had once teased his envy now struck him as oddly tedious. Zip ignored the hubbub by default, content to march forward without distraction. Roy studied his partner's stride, finally realizing that the snazzy duds were little more than a clever disguise.

Zip ducked behind a familiar kiosk and into a dim service tunnel. Roy followed him inside, maintaining a close proximity. The squishing bag caught his attention again. He eyed the duffle and cringed at the unpleasant sound. It wasn't laundry. That he knew. But what he really wanted to know was ... scratch that. He didn't want to know.

A sharp ping echoed inside the tunnel. Roy patted his chest and pants before fishing his comdev from a rear pocket. *Probably Duncan checking in,* he thought. He tapped the screen, read the message, and stopped dead in his tracks.

Zip noticed that he was alone after a few steps, forcing him to stop and turn to a bewildered Roy. The bag sloshed as he sighed and backtracked to his partner. "What's wrong?" he said with a hint of annoyance.

Roy stared at his comdev in disbelief. "I, um ..."

"Spit it out, plumber. We don't have all day."

"I'm ... *rich.*"

"Huh?"

"I just received a deposit for 250,000 credits. Look." Roy flipped the screen to Zip.

Zip shrugged. "Yeah, so? That's your payment for the job."

"*Really?* This is more than I earn in a *decade.*"

"Sounds like you have a shitty career."

Roy stuttered in response, waffling between shock and offense.

"Listen," Zip said with a more affable tone. "Werner is one of the most powerful beings in the universe. He controls a level of wealth that you and I can only dream of. He could wipe his ass with that payment and never miss it. And besides, you just pulled his ass from the proverbial fire. All of our asses, for that matter. You earned every cent of that bounty. If anything, you were underpaid." Zip turned away and continued his trek down the tunnel.

A wide grin stretched across Roy's face. He glanced at his comdev, huffed with immense satisfaction, then jogged to catch up.

* * *

I watched with fascination as another guard set a fresh cup of tea on the table next to Zip, along with a small assortment of sugars and creamers. This from a corrections officer with a plasma weapon attached to his belt.

I had officially entered Opposite Land.

Review: a strange and perilous place where armored guards serve afternoon tea to serial killers. Intriguing, but not recommended.

"Thank you, Milo," Zip said. "Hellos to the wife and kids."

The guard bowed like a tip-starved waiter and took his leave. Zip dressed the tea, took a sip, then gestured for me to continue. I sat on the opposite side of a security table. He was chained to the floor with titanium shackles, and yet, I sensed that he was in full control of my impunity. But alas, the show (or unfolding hostage situation) must go on.

If you hated Roy so much, then why offer the encouragement?

Like I said, he was very good at what he did. Werner liked him, which meant that Gamon was gonna keep using him. Which *also* meant that I was likely to continue working with him.

Which you did, I presume.

Yes. We returned to The Craven Compass and met with Gamon. As suspected, it was a giant circle jerk of praise and back-patting. Gamon's rep was on the line, so the whole thing ended with a giant sigh of relief. Roy had scored big out of the gate, which inflated his ego a bit. He didn't know how rare of an occurrence that was, so I had to temper his arrogance from time to time. I served as a pseudo mentor on recurring jobs. Granted, they all required my expertise in cold-blooded murder.

(Ping. "Haha, he does love that nickname for graffiti.")

Roy remained blissfully obtuse. Most of my work resided in the background. He'd work a problem while I ducked away to slit a throat.

(Ping. "Spray some paint.")

You know, it's interesting. I spent a great deal of time piecing this all together. I studied hours upon hours of Roy's numerous exploits. I watched you both, along with a host of other characters, wandering in and out of precarious situations throughout the station. And not once did I see any evidence of your ... let's say, special abilities.

I don't think that's interesting at all. Not to point out the obvious, but concealing evidence is kind of a prerequisite for what I do.

No, you misunderstand. I was paying you a compliment. In combing the security footage, I only witnessed a single blunder. And, as a not-so-subtle observation, it was the only event in which you were notably absent.

The casino job.

Yes. Can you tell me more about that?

Well, like you said, I wasn't there. I was in the room when it was issued, but further details are foggy at best. However, I *can* tell you why the evidence is out in the open.

And why's that?

Because Durangoni was the benefactor.

(Ping. "Fake news.")

CHAPTER 12

Gamon lit a fresh cigar from his comfy chair behind a large wooden desk. Puffs of smoke floated through the dim room. It was a different desk inside a different location, but carried the same seedy vibe. Gamon's dealings required a certain amount of mobility, but at the same time, he also valued cohesion. Whenever he held a meeting, one could expect a cloud of cigar smoke and a big damn desk.

Zip stood over his shoulder, as always, maintaining his best "normal guy and definitely not a murderous hitman" persona. Roy sat in one of two chairs in front of the desk, playing a mental game of "spot the difference" from The Craven Compass. Wallpaper darker, floor space bigger, folding chairs needlessly uncomfortable. Annoying squeaks accented his every movement. He thought about complaining, but opted to remain calm and stoic.

"These chairs suck," he said to Gamon.

"What are you, the chair police?"

Zip rolled his eyes.

Moments later, the entry door whipped open and bounced off the wall, drawing flinches from everyone inside. Vierra Belliosa marched into the room and slammed the door behind her. Her dreads were pulled into a tight ponytail. A large pair of sunglasses concealed much of her face. She plucked them off and hooked them to her blouse, a frilly purple bodice that matched her skirt and satchel. In a single fluid motion, she plunked into the vacant chair and crossed one leg over the other.

Roy smiled at her blunt arrival. His chest swelled with adoration, as she was even more enchanting than he remembered.

Vierra dropped her satchel to the floor and noticed Roy sitting beside her. She mirrored his smile and offered a fist-bump. "Eeey, Roy m'boy."

"Great to see you, Vee," he said, completing the bump.

Their attention turned to Gamon, who eyed them both through a haze of impatience.

Gamon released a puff of smoke. "Thank you for finally gracing us with your presence. We've only been sitting here for half an hour."

"Fuck off, hairball. I had a thing."

Roy smirked, which Zip caught from afar. And then Roy caught Zip's resulting scowl, which immediately erased the smirk.

Vierra twirled an arm. "I'm here. Chop chop."

Gamon sighed and swallowed his retort, as Belliosa remained one of the very few who could address him with such brashness. In any other situation, Zip would already be in the process of removing her head. "Okay, so, this job is going to sound a little strange. But before I get into the details, please rest assured that there is no foul play afoot. We are in no danger. We are not being watched, nor are any of us being squeezed in any way."

Vierra narrowed her eyes. "That's not as reassuring as you think it is."

"Given the nature of the assignment, the preface should make sense."

Vierra sighed, then gestured to continue.

Roy shifted a concerned gaze between the two.

"We've been asked to shake down the Zandui Casino."

Vierra burst into laughter, slapped her knees, then leapt to her feet. She shook her head as if to say *you dumb hairy bastard*, then hooked her satchel and drifted towards the exit. "And who, pray tell, is this astoundingly stupid backer?"

"The Durangoni Space Station," Gamon said with a flat tone. Vierra stopped in her tracks and whipped a stunned gaze to the beast. "Are you fucking kidding me?"

Gamon shook his head.

"Why in the fucking fuck of fuck would you solicit a job from the very entity that you are hiding jobs from?"

"I didn't," Gamon said, adding a shrug. "They approached me."

The statement smacked Vierra across the face, rendering her speechless. She thought for a moment, then about-faced and shuffled back to her seat. Her bum met the rickety chair without breaking eye contact.

"Durangoni caught Zandui funneling massive sums of money to the Varokins."

Vierra huffed and fell back in her chair. "Fuuuck a ferret."

"To who?" Roy said.

"A massive sect of organized crime," Gamon said to Roy. "The Varokin Empire controls the Black Razor fleet and most of the abyssal markets. Normally, Durangoni would purge the casino and install someone else. But, Zandui is the biggest name in the game. They generate more cash than the next dozen combined. And so, Durangoni has found itself in quite the pickle."

"So what's the play?"

"They want us to hack into the Zandui financial block." Gamon nodded at Vierra. "You specifically, and then redirect the Varokin funds to Durangoni charities. The only catch is, they want it done from *inside* the casino."

Vierra cocked an eyebrow. "What the hell for?"

Gamon retrieved a note from a side drawer and placed it face-up on the desk. He pressed a finger to the paper and slid it over to Roy and Vierra. "This is their offer."

They leaned in for a gander.

"Sweet Tim almighty," Roy said. "That's a *lot* of zeroes."

"Not to them," Gamon said.

"He's right," Vierra said, then glanced at Roy. "This isn't about the money. It's about saving face. Corruption at that level undermines their credibility. They can't shut Zandui down without looking like fools."

"Bingo," Gamon said. "Durangoni *wants* Zandui to see this. They *want* them to see the fix, and they *want* them to know that it was Vierra Belliosa. It would send a clear message that they have the eyes and power, but also value stability. The casino would have no choice but to keep the fix in place, lest they suffer a very public scandal."

"Like a penalty tax," Roy said.

"Exactly," Gamon said.

"So why not do it themselves?"

"Same problem," Vierra said. "Durangoni officials shaking down a casino would not go over well in the public eye. The station prides itself on unrestricted commerce. The second they install anything that resembles a tax, the merchants would revolt."

Gamon click-pointed at Vierra.

"And what if I say no?"

"Umm ..." Gamon said, taken aback. "You're ... disinterested?"

"Oh, no, I'm definitely doing it. Sounds like a cracker. However, given that they want *me* specifically, I was wondering what their Plan B was."

Gamon scrunched his brow and rapped his meaty fingers on the desk. The cigar migrated back and forth between his lips. He examined the offer note like a smarmy professor grading a subpar paper. "I believe their Plan B would be to devise a Plan B."

Vierra chuckled. "Sounds about right."

Roy raised his hand and immediately spoke, negating the hand raise. "So where do I fit in with all this?"

"You're her husband," Gamon said, gesturing at Vierra.

"If only," Roy said with a sheepish chuckle. The reply was somewhat involuntary, which infected the group with a twinge of awkwardness.

"No," Gamon said. "You will be playing a married couple in order to gain access to the casino. To be fair, Vierra could rock into the place by herself and sling some code, but we want to eliminate as much suspicion as we can. At least, up to the point of hacking. And so, you will both get dressed to impress, visit the casino like any normal couple with money to burn, find a nice cozy table, order a steak, eat the steak, then whip out a tablet and get to work. That should give you enough time to complete the assignment before they wise up."

"And what if we get caught?" Roy said.

Gamon narrowed his gaze. "That's the point, dingus."

Zip rolled his eyes again.

"No," Roy said. "I mean, what if Vierra needs more time?"

"Then *you* provide it. Your job is to run interference, should it be necessary."

"Gotcha." Roy gave Gamon a thumbs-up, then smiled at Vierra.

"I'll do some digging and have everything primed beforehand," Vierra said. "Shouldn't take long once we're inside, just a quick log and load. The only x-factor will be the number of funnels I have to route."

"And what happens when the job is done?" Roy said.

Gamon shrugged. "Get up and walk out."

"Sorry, but, um," Roy said, clearly stumped. "Won't they want to detain us? Question us? Or at the very least, track us once we leave?"

Gamon thought for a moment while chewing on his cigar. "Who is the most famous person you can think of?"

"Kirp Delon." (Read: the quadrant equivalent of Tom Hanks.)

"Okay, so, let's say that you're having breakfast at home. It's a normal day, normal routine, nothing amiss or out of place. Then, Kirp Delon walks into the room. You didn't even know he was in your house. Without a word, he climbs onto the table, drops his pants, shits on your plate, wipes his ass with your napkin, and then smears it on your face before taking his leave. At that moment, would you be worried about tracking him, or would you be utterly paralyzed by what the fuck just happened?"

Roy thought hard about the visual while pulling his gaze around the group. His face cycled between shock, disgust, and total bewilderment. The more he envisioned the act, the more his stomach churned. It all ended with a clumsy dry-heave.

Zip facepalmed himself.

* * *

Vierra watched with great amusement as the bartender poured our fifth shots of rum. At least, that's what they called it. To be perfectly honest, it tasted like the hateful backwash of a demonic enema. As a wandering haze engulfed my field of vision, I was never more thankful for the audio recorder on my comdev.

Puki Horpocket was not a big drinker.

Puki Horpocket was decidedly smashed.

Nevertheless, I persisted.

We toasted to our health (ironically) and tossed back another round of taint juice.

(cough) Sweet mercy.

Way to keep up, wordsmith. Most lightweights would have tapped out by now.

Was that the (cough) intention?

Nah. I just wanted to see how badly you wanted this interview.

Diabolic. But I respect it.

And I respect your tenacity. Please continue, if you can.

So you and Roy (hiccup) inflo ... infur ... infiltrated the Zandui Casino.

Yes, but it was scarcely an infiltration. We just walked through the front doors like every other deep pocket. I will say this, though. Roy was quite the gentleman and walking into Zandui was the closest I ever felt to being a princess.

* * *

When it comes to the Zandui Casino, the word is *extravagance.* While an abundance of swanky haunts is scattered throughout the station, Zandui remains the only public venue that thrills with each visit. I have dined at several of its five-star restaurants in order to revise entries in the Definitive Directory of Durangoni, and those experiences barely scratch the surface. The casino is a veritable theme park for anyone with a swollen bank account.

First of all, Zandui is big. Like, *really* big. It's essentially a giant pleasure cruiser built into the northernmost Rich Ring. It spans 15 floors and covers an area the size of a pomplomo pitch (read: about eight football fields). It houses more hotels, pubs, and restaurants than most actual districts, as well as several premium theaters and playhouses. It even has its own docking portal and full-time valet service. In fact, it's not uncommon for bigwigs to visit the station for months and never leave the casino grounds.

And then there is the casino itself.

Describing the main gaming floor is a somewhat daunting task. It remains one of the few sights aboard the station that drops my jaw. The enormous open space spans ten stories with high-roller tables littering the floor. Countless balconies overlook the action, which remain in near-constant use. This is due to a never-ending holographic spectacle that fills the open space. Sometimes it's a mass of floating orbs set to trippy music. Other times, it's a flock of rainbow dragons pooping fireworks. It's a ceaseless and utterly dazzling light show, one you could stalk for weeks and never see the same thing twice.

Regardless of location, casino sounds are always needling the background. Clinking glasses, clacking chips, the occasional roar of big wins. The entire place is an unremitting churn, always on, never placid. And yet, within this restless arena, Roy and Vierra somehow managed to steal the spotlight. At least, ever so briefly.

* * *

Roy stood inside a restaurant lobby on the third level, adjusting to his tuxedo rental. He had worn one back on his home planet, but the Durangoni upgrade took some getting used to. It was not uncomfortable, but rather *too* comfortable. Roy was so attuned to poverty rags that his body outright rejected form-fitted clothing. A reception booth faced a pair of elevator doors. Elegant folk arrived with each ding and were guided into the establishment by one of several uniformed hosts. Roy watched them all through an odd sense of discomfort. Not from the attire, but from a chronic dysphoria. Most of his life aboard the station had been spent in filthy dives. Whenever he met eyes with a host, he braced himself to be shooed away like an unwelcome pest.

Another ding of arrival caught his attention. He turned to the elevator doors, which slid open to reveal an enchanting woman dressed in a shimmering gown. The silky fabric clung to a single shoulder and draped across her chest, giving her the presence of a debutante. Glittering earrings peeked through her black dreads, all carefully teased into a stylish bun. Her heels clacked to a rest in front of Roy, drawing a wide smile across his face.

"My stars, are you a vision to behold," he said.

"Thanks," Vierra said with a playful smirk. "And you're looking quite dapper, mister man. C'mon, give momma a spin."

Roy struck a butler-like pose and twisted in a slow circle.

"Yes, yes, very nice, liking that," she said while nodding.

Roy ended with an outstretched elbow and a toothy grin. "Shall we, m'lady?"

She chuckled and hooked her arm around his, painting the intended portrait.

They moseyed up to the reception booth where a uniformed hostess escorted them into the ritzy restaurant. A faint and pleasant melody welcomed them, serving as a backdrop to cultured conversation. Fine silver rested atop round tables with white coverings. Intricate patterns adorned the walls and ceiling, all illuminated by crystal sconces and chandeliers. Roy smiled as his gaze wandered freely, lost in a sea of opulence.

The hostess presented their table, a private two-seater on its own balcony overlooking the casino. Holographic ribbons twisted around the interior as a muted roar lifted from the gaming floor. Roy and Vierra took their seats, allowing the hostess to bow and take her leave. A suited waiter arrived with a pair of complementary martinis, a tasty house spirit that tempted longer stays. After reciting the specials with pitch-perfect charm, he logged their orders and whisked away like an elvish prince.

Roy and Vierra lifted their glasses and toasted to friendship. They mused on their extralegal adventures, prompting several laughs and sighs. For once, they were able to indulge in personal quirks. Roy learned that Vierra loved tabletop puzzles. Vierra learned that Roy could recite the entire Garlokian Pledge (a statement of loyalty that was widely considered a masterpiece of empty rhetoric). The occasional roar of victory pulled their attention to the gaming floor where boisterous moguls splashed cash around high-stakes tables. The gathered crowds cheered every play like traveling entourages.

"So I have to ask," Roy said. "Why hasn't anyone mobbed you?"

"What do you mean?"

"You are crazy famous throughout Durangoni. If Kirp Delon were to walk in here, he would draw immediate attention from staff and fans. You're arguably more famous than he is, so where are all the groupies?"

"The difference is, Kirp is a famous actor. I'm a famous engineer."

"So?"

"So, you know my work, not my face. When you first met me at the Sunken Isles, did you recognize me?"

"No."

"But you knew my name."

"Yes."

"There you have it."

"But still, you'd think at least someone in-the-know would be fawning over you."

"Ah, that's because I go to great pains to conceal my public identity. Well, not so much conceal. More like overload with false positives."

"How so?"

"See for yourself. Grab your comdev search for my name."

Roy complied. A quick search returned a smorgasbord of non-Vierras. Face after face of random people, all linked to various articles about her exploits. Many claimed to be the "real" Vierra, yet none of them was. It took a solid minute of scrolling before Roy found a matching image, and even that was just a candid picture with no context. "That's astounding."

"True privacy is only found in chaos. I learned early on that it's easier to hide in bad data. Why fight the system when you can turn it against itself?"

"That's damn near poetic."

"Psh. I suck at poetry."

"Somehow I doubt that."

Vierra smiled and added a flirtatious wink.

The waiter returned and lowered two plates to the table, both cragono steaks, another shared interest they had uncovered. Roy followed her lead, selecting the same pieces of silverware that she did. They moaned with culinary pleasure while trading coy glances. Every morsel a delight, every moment a treasure. A strange sensation bubbled inside his stomach. It was wholly foreign, yet oddly fulfilling.

Roy was ... *happy*.

A sudden commotion from the gaming floor caught their attention. Roy craned his neck over the balcony to find a large rectangular pane suspended over a ticketing booth. It was filled with glowing numbers, similar to a bingo board, but bizarrely random. The crowd had moaned with disappointment and began to disperse. Moments later, the board cleared itself for another round. A small bulb in the upper corner started to blink in peculiar intervals. Roy studied it with intense fascination.

"What is that blinking light?" he said.

Vierra glanced at the board. "You mean the Big Sixty counter?"

"What's that?"

"You've never heard of Big Sixty?"

"No. Is it fun?"

"Fun?" she said with a slight chuckle. "It's simultaneously the most unwinnable and irresistible game in all of existence. The cost is huge and the payoff is absurd. It's a sucker's paradise that makes a shit-ton of money for the casino. In fact, I would wager that Big Sixty is their primary source of revenue."

"What are the rules?"

Vierra narrowed her eyes. "You've seriously never heard of this?"

Roy shrugged. "Well, we play it all the time down in the subcore. Just making sure that *you* understand it."

"Smartass. But point taken."

"C'mon, humor me. How does it work?"

"You're not going to play it." Vierra sipped her martini.

"I'm just curious," Roy said with a glib tone. "I lucked my way out of crippling poverty to relax inside a prestigious casino with the most beautiful woman I have ever known. Trust me, I am not eager to goad my karma."

Vierra smiled and blushed a bit. "Okay, but promise me. Not one ticket."

"Promise." Roy circled his spleen. (Read: crossed his heart. This was a cultural gesture that even Vierra found confusing. She snorted with amusement, then continued.)

"Alright, so, Big Sixty is a simple guessing game. There are sixty squares, each representing a minute of the current hour. The object of the game is to guess the number for each square. Players purchase tickets, log their guesses, and submit them before the hour begins. A random number is revealed each minute, ranging from zero to a hundred. If you guess them all, you win."

Roy pondered the rules for a moment, then tilted his head. "What moron would ever play such a stupid game?"

"Exactly. The odds are astronomical. But then there's the payoff."

"Must be pretty big to get dumb people to flush money down the toilet."

"Three hundred trillion credits."

Roy flinched into stunned silence. He could only stare at Vierra through a haze of disbelief. His brain inputted the figure, but locked up and sent a critical error to his mouth hole. "*What?!*" he said with a mixture of shock, anger, and a bit of arousal.

Vierra grinned and nodded.

"*What?!*" he said again, adding a table slap.

"Now you get it."

"Sweet Tim almighty."

"I know, right? The game is unwinnable, but the pot is why people play. And here's the kicker. Each ticket costs 10,000 credits."

Roy twitched in response, as his brain had no idea what else to do.

"And even at that price point, there are thousands of tickets played every hour."

Roy leaned back and crossed his arms. "Are you messing with me? You have to be messing with me."

"Ten thousand credits to win three hundred trillion? When you have money to burn, it doesn't seem so reckless, does it?"

"It has to be a scam. No way that game is legit."

"I thought so too, but the algorithm was verified by seven independent bodies. No tricks, no scam, just a near-impossible puzzle. And get this, the casino actually encourages players to try and crack the code. Professional gamblers have been running the numbers for decades. Even the most sophisticated code breakers haven't been able to crack that nut. I've been tempted to give it a go myself, but countless people, intelligent people, have gone broke trying."

"Wait, did you say *decades?*"

"Yup. Big Sixty has been around since I was a kid, and the jackpot has yet to be won. Think about that. Ten thousand credits per ticket, thousands of plays per hour, over *decades.*"

Roy leaned forward and rubbed the hurt from his temples.

"That's the kind of monetary flow we're dealing with." Her tone switched from somber to peppy. "And I'm about to hack that shit." She reached into her purse, withdrew a small tablet, and plunked it on the table.

CHAPTER 13

Despite the supervillain level of techno malfeasance occurring at the other side of the table, Roy was oddly relaxed. He munched on his delectable steak, sipped his delicious martini, and watched the colorful light show twist and turn over the balcony. A cheeky grin stretched across his face as he watched a school of hologram fish swim above the casino floor. They glided over the Big Sixty booth, switching his focus to the algorithm counter.

Roy stared at the light for what seemed like an eternity. The pulses teased his conscience, scratching a familiar yet distant itch.

Minute by minute, the blinking light morphed into a beating drum. The little voice inside his head grew louder and louder. He wondered if their digital raid could be viewed as malfeasance if the governing party was the actual government. And then he wondered if the government would protect them should the job go off the rails. And then he wondered who around him was a secret agent waiting to slit his throat after the job was done. What had started as a subtle worry was building into a full-blown conspiracy panic.

"Nervous?" Vierra said without looking up from the tablet.

Roy noticed that he was holding his breath. He released the pent-up air and ended with a shy chuckle. "Is it that obvious?"

"Lil' bit."

"Sorry."

"Don't be," she said while tapping. "If anything, it makes us look like a married couple with unresolved issues."

"How so?"

"Well, we're at a fancy dinner and I'm nose-deep in a tablet. You're acting all weird, like you just confessed to something. I wager that everyone around us thinks you're having an affair."

Roy gasped. "I would never do that to you."

Vierra snorted. "Way to sell it."

"Oh ... yeah." Roy blushed and cleared his throat.

She smirked and tossed him a glance. "Don't worry, I'm almost done here."

"Must be pretty complicated."

"Not really. I finished the hack five minutes ago."

"You fin—*what?*"

"The reroute was super easy. I researched all the funnel points beforehand and had the protocols ready to go. Hacked in, ran the script, *boom.*"

Roy stammered in reply. "So what the hell have you been doing?"

Vierra stopped tapping and gave her full attention to Roy. She took a needed breath as her cavalier demeanor switched to a somber tone. "Once I gained access to the Zandui network, I needed to answer a very important question."

"And what's that?" he said, matching her earnestness.

Vierra nodded, allowing the gravity of the predicament to settle between them. "I needed to know ... " She paused for weight. "Could I hack into the hologram control system and force it to render photoreal pornography?"

Roy responded with a blank stare.

"The answer," she said, switching back to peppy, "is a resounding *yes.*" She waved a finger over the tablet and dropped it onto the screen.

The hologram show crackled and disappeared.

The music stopped.

The roar of conversation faded.

From the depths of oblivion, a smooth and seductive beat filled the empty space. And then the hologram system got down to business, in more ways than one. It created image after image of hardcore alien debauchery. Couples, threesomes, and outright orgies entangled each other in lustful abandon. Their naked bodies towered over the space, plunging every throbbing limb into every gaping hole. Flesh jiggled. Sacks dangled. Juices spilled from moist cavities. Gasps lifted from the gaming floor as shocked patrons sidestepped the rendered fluids.

Every eye inside the casino locked onto the show.

Most jaws dangled in stunned silence.

Roy's was one of them.

Other jaws formed wide smiles of approval.

Vierra's was one of them.

She chuckled at the sultry tableau. "Is it weird to be aroused by this?"

Roy turned his befuddled gaze to Vierra.

"You know what this needs?"

Roy responded by not responding.

"Blongos," she said with excitement, then tapped the screen again.

(Blongos can best be described as highly aggressive, yet oddly adorable goat-like creatures. They are prized as pets due to their superior home-guarding skills, but will often trash the place with their comically large horns, which somewhat negates burglary.)

Out of nowhere, a giant herd of blongos invaded the pornographic wonderland. A chorus of "awww" lifted from the crowd, but was soon quashed when the creatures decided to join the party. Their massive members hunted for any crevice that would accept them. Howls of success married into the moans of pleasure. A few critters preferred to bash each other with their giant horns, accenting the erotic music with violent clunks.

Vierra added claps to her chuckles. "Oh wow, that is balls-out brilliant," she said with several balls swinging overhead. "This might be some of my finest work."

"Ahem," said a nearby voice.

Roy and Vierra turned to find three casino guards blocking the exit from their booth. Not Durangoni Security officers, just three random aliens with blue uniforms and rent-a-badges. The head guard puffed his chest and glowered at Vierra. "You need to come with us, ma'am," he said with a slightly threatening tone.

"Pass," she said.

"E—excuse me?"

"That's a hard no, pal. And for that matter, how the fuck did you even know I was here? I killed the relay trackers, and it's not like there's a ping-trace on the holo—" Her eyes narrowed with realization. "Aaaah, fuck all of you right in the neck."

"Not playing games, ma'am." The guard stepped towards her and motioned to rise. "Please come with us. I will not ask again."

Vierra huffed and turned to Roy. "You're up, partner."

"Uuuh ..." Roy said through his dangling jaw.

"Your job is to run interference. Sooo ..." She gestured to the guards.

Roy looked at the guards, then back to Vierra, then back to the guards, then up to the moist genitals overhead, then back to Vierra.

Vierra sighed with disappointment.

The guard reached for her shoulder, but met a sudden resistance. He looked down to see Roy's hand clamped around his wrist. Anger swelled inside his chest. His gaze crawled up the limb to Roy's face, where a pair of clouded eyes glared back at him. Roy grumbled as noxious spit dribbled from his frothing mouth. The guard yelped and snatched his arm away, stumbling back into one of his cohorts.

Vierra's eyes widened.

"Meet me back at the elevator," Roy said under his breath, then slowly rose from his seat.

The guards braced themselves as a snarling beast in a rented tuxedo stood from the table and turned to face them. Its pupils were lost beneath a milky haze. Acidic slobber pooled on the floor. Roy hunched his back and grunted like a rabid werewolf.

At this point, everyone inside the dining room had given Roy their undivided attention, despite the hologram orgy raging overhead. One of the guards stammered through his waning authority. "Sir, please put away the ... um, stop doing, uh ... stop being weird, sir."

Roy whipped his clouded gaze to the frightened guard, flinging ribbons of spit across the floor. The guard squeaked and took a wary step back. Roy grumbled with ferocity, prompting nearby diners to abandon their tables.

Roy stepped forward.

The guards stepped back.

Roy stepped forward.

The guards—

Roy shrieked and rushed the guards.

All three yelped, spun around, and sprinted away in different directions. The remaining diners screamed and fled their tables, creating a cauldron of chaos inside the restaurant.

Roy slid to a halt outside the booth and snarled while snapping his gaze between the fleeing guards. Frothy spit poured from his mouth with each whip and grunt. He selected a guard, then raised his arms overhead and gave chase like a hungry goblin.

Vierra snickered as she tucked the tablet into her purse. She rose from the table, straightened her dress, then strolled away as a feast of sexual conquest played in the background.

* * *

The restaurant lobby had cleared out, leaving some lingering staff and a small group of casino guards. Roy entered through a side door, having reset the froth monster and regained some normalcy. Aside from a few lapel stains (which guaranteed the loss of his deposit), his secret identity remained hidden. He twisted around the lobby in search of Vierra, but she was nowhere to be found.

And then he heard her voice.

He struggled to pinpoint the location and eventually settled on the guards. A different lot from the chase, but the same uniforms and lack of authority. They had surrounded someone. A very special someone. Roy caught a glimpse of her gown from within the mass, then readied himself for another frothy attack. But as he started to churn his gut, Vierra's signature cackle erupted from the group. The guards followed suit, matching her laugh in tone and delight. Roy halted the boil and relaxed his stomach, opting to approach with caution. The footsteps caught the attention of the nearest guard, who politely stepped aside to reveal Vierra.

She was signing autographs.

Roy released a heavy sigh.

Vierra met his gaze and replied with a smile. "Okay boys, that's enough." She clapped and shooed the guards away. "Go do whatever you should be doing."

They all groaned and slinked away, albeit with wide grins on their faces. After all, it's not every day that you get to meet a living legend. They ignored Roy altogether and vanished back into the casino.

Roy took his final steps and settled in front of Vierra.

"Well that was an interesting exit," she said with a slight chuckle. "But I gotta hand it to you, it's a very effective strategy."

Roy smiled and shrugged. "Learned it as a child, been using it ever since. Comes in handy from time to time."

"Smells like ass, though."

"Kinda the point, like when animals use musk to deter predators. My species isn't exactly known for their burly frames." Roy offered a meager flex, then waved it away.

"Oh, I get it. Doesn't make it any less funky."

Roy grinned, then retrieved a small bottle of mouthwash from his pocket. He took a swig, then sloshed it around and swallowed. "Never leave home without it."

Vierra smirked. "Roy, m'boy, did you just freshen up for a nightcap?"

Of course he didn't, but she didn't know that. And so began a vicious mental game of *tell the truth, no, lie, no, tell the truth, no, lie.*

She lightly punched his shoulder. "Kidding, dude."

Roy simpered and glanced away.

"Great work today," she said with a coy tone.

"You too. I'm still trying to get those blongos out of my head."

She chuckled softly and ended with a sigh. "I guess this is good-bye, then."

"Guess so."

Vierra patted his chest, then turned for the elevator and pressed the call button. A ping replied and the doors slid open. Roy watched with great affection as she stepped into the car and turned to face him. They traded playful smirks as the doors began to close.

But then she reached out and stopped them.

Roy cocked his brow.

"You coming or not?" she said.

He smiled wide and joined her.

* * *

There have been a few low points in my life, the majority of which will remain locked away in the basement of shame. However, in order to complete this tale of intrigue, I must confess to an event that I am none too proud of.

During my interview with Vierra Belliosa, she succeeded in pushing my drinking limit to an embarrassing new level. After an obscene amount of rum shots, we had to cut the interview short because, and these are her words, I was "dancing along the beach like a circus performer caught in a violent hallucination." Apparently, I had to be wrangled several times until I passed out in a lounge chair.

The next morning, I awoke in the same chair.

Vierra had shielded my limp body from the beating sun with a canopy of umbrellas. As my eyes opened, my brain declared its utter displeasure with the situation. My head was pounding, my mouth was parched, and my pants remain missing to this day. There is something unsettling about a man wearing a suit jacket with socks and boxers. Especially on the beach. But that's how the interview resumed, and I owned it for the remainder.

Vierra was lounging in the adjacent chair when I awoke. She had changed into a one-piece swimsuit with a matching sash and hat. The sun reflected off her larger-than-life sunglasses. She looked happy, healthy, and clear-headed, an image that I greatly coveted at that moment. As she explained, "Hangovers are not a thing with me." I still wonder what she meant. Was it a *species* thing or a *supernatural tolerance* thing? I decided not to press, because any further talk of booze would have purged what little remained in my stomach.

Speaking of which, she was kind enough to order breakfast for the both of us. Few things are better for a raging hangover than a hot plate of forfum, shanwap, and a tall glass of gurpoonga. (Read: pass. Some things need a translation. This plate of horrors does not. In fact, learning what this was prompted a two-week hiatus where I almost quit the project.)

We ate our breakfast, exchanged some repartee, and picked up where we left off the night before. Vierra detailed the hack job and took great pleasure in highlighting the most salacious tidbits. I hung on her every word while trying not to vomit.

To be honest, I am surprised that Gamon would sign off on such a plan.

Goodness, no. He had no idea. The whole orgy thing was my own added flair.

Seems a bit cavalier, don't you think?

The casino funded terrorists. I would happily take the lumps for twisting that knife. In fact, I bricked the debug console and tanked the resets. The holo-orgy ran for an entire week before they threw in the towel and wiped the system. That was a mountain of dirty money down the shitter, thanks to yours truly.

What did Gamon say about it?

Tore me a new one, which I richly deserved. Haven't worked with him since. But that's okay, I'm much happier on my own.

And what about Roy?

(slight pause, then shrugs) What about him?

Have you seen or worked with him since?

Roy continued to work for Gamon, as far as I know. I didn't hear much about his whereabouts until the snafu leading up to The Incident. Got a ring-ding out of the blue.

He reached out to you.

Yes.

What about?

He had gotten into a bind and needed some guidance. And *that*, Mr. Horpocket, is as far as I'm willing to take you.

Understood. But if you would be so kind, I do have one last question.

Shoot.

I have studied this event from every angle, from beginning to end, but you and Roy entering the elevator remains the last piece of footage I can find. In fact, I discovered that an entire sequence was missing from the security archives. If I had to wager a guess, I think that Durangoni erased them to conceal your departure.

Seems reasonable, but I'm not hearing a question.

I would like to know where you went.

(smirks) Somewhere private.

Care to elaborate?

Nope.

Fair enough. And, if you will, one final, final question.

(brief chuckle) You're a pushy little prick fuck, you know that?

I've been told, yes.

Okay then. One more. Consider it a hangover gift.

Thank you, dear. I just want to know, for the sake of my own curiosity ... were you surprised when Roy won the Big Sixty jackpot?

No.

Wow. Was not expecting so quick an answer.

(shrugs) It was Roy's to win. He noticed the one thing that nobody else did. And I can think of no one more deserving.

* * *

I departed shortly after breakfast and never saw Vierra again.

It was sad in a way, as her immense persona enters a room long before she does. She's a living legend, a roving apparition that continues to improve our strange and wonderful world. Ironic, given her distaste for the celebrity it bestows.

Vierra provided valuable clues into Roy's final days before The Incident. After our meeting, I realized that I was crafting a story of redemption. Roy was not a villain. He was neither luminary nor enigma. He was a good man, as she insisted.

Roy was a cog.

A cog that wished to be a lever.

And that lever would move the world.

CHAPTER 14

After numerous interviews with Roy's inner circle, I had enough puzzle pieces to begin constructing his meteoric rise into the public conscience. I had examined Roy the grunt and followed his choppy path to Roy the crook, a humble dreg in the throes of a midlife crisis. In another world, on another station, the tale of a working stiff winning an unwinnable fortune would be enough to sell a pile of hardbacks. But life inside Durangoni is a unique brand of vagary. It's filled with special stories about special people doing remarkably special things.

The time has come to reveal Roy the folk hero.

The time has come to address The Incident.

The following is a dramatic reconstruction of the events leading up to Roy's mysterious departure from the station. It is a conjecture based on interviews, security reels, and reams of hearsay. While some details may not be entirely accurate, I stand by the depiction as a faithful and thoughtful retelling.

* * *

Roy sat inside his tiny apartment, trying his best to ignore the funk and racket. Months had passed since he departed, yet there he was, a stranger in his own strange land. The ratty cot was painfully uncomfortable, especially compared to the fluffy beds he enjoyed on assignment. Even the worst outing was vastly superior to his shabby bunk down in the sub-core.

And yet, it felt like home.

He patted the frame like an old friend, then refocused on the opposite wall, the same soiled pane where he composed a message to Gamon. He traced a scratch over to a set of wire hangers clinging to dents in the metal. Dirty clothes hung from their frames, each stain telling a woeful tale. He could smell the grease, taste the brine, hear the clanks of hammers. His gaze fell to his lap, where a pair of fine slacks covered his thighs. A single square inch of that fabric cost more than the entirety of his sub-core belongings.

He had everything he wanted, and yet, nothing at all.

Gamon had released him for several days, as nothing on the docket warranted his skill set. Roy had become a favorite lackey, due to his unique ability to address complex problems while not resembling a complex being. Gamon loved having a forgettable technician at his disposal, which afforded Roy lots of interesting work. And as a result, lots of disposable income.

When Roy received a long-overdue break, he decided to treat himself for the first time since leaving his homeworld. Using Zip's fashionable insight, he purchased a new set of clothes from the same shopping district where he had fixed the clogged fountains. He felt like a million bucks when he left the store. But when he returned home, he felt like a thief.

Roy rolled the fabric between his fingertips and finally understood the dilemma that Clancy faced every day. Rich on paper, poor inside, a bottomless hole to fill. A rush of guilt infected his conscience. Clancy never deserved the abuse, no matter how thick the veneer of envy.

What a shitty friend I've been.

With a heavy sigh, Roy stood from the cot and turned for the door. His somber gaze crept around the tiny abode one last time before taking his leave.

The sights and sounds of a returning shift filled the cramped hallway. Roy sidestepped his former compatriots, who paid him no mind. Not a single grunt recognized him. Their curious eyes stopped at his slacks and dismissed him as a rich wanker who lost his way. Roy sighed into a knowing nod, having replaced his comfort with chagrin. He scanned the mass for his long-time mates, none of whom revealed themselves. His wandering gaze landed on Duncan's apartment, but there was no need to visit. Roy knew exactly where he was.

It was time for a drink.

Roy strolled back to the nearest pod station where a group of grunts awaited the next train. He kept his distance, opting to wait behind them. A few tossed him sour glances, even meeting eyes for a moment, but still failed to recognize him. Roy glanced down at his tidy shirt, which may as well have been a cloak of invisibility.

The ride up to the merchant line was a similar bout of indignation. Roy bit his tongue and bided his time as the group mumbled about the cleaner-than-usual passenger. They poked fun at his shiny shoes, custom belt, and willful use of soap. Roy heard none of this, but understood the mannerisms. After all, he knew them as his own.

The pod train slowed to a stop and released its cargo into the merchant district. Roy made his way through a noisy bazaar of practical shops. He recognized them all and could even name the vendors, but none of them offered anything of interest. His trained eyes could spot deals across the lot, but he ignored them all as beneath regard. Grease was now an obstacle to avoid. Clanks were now curses that abhorred his presence.

Roy proceeded into a far corridor and ducked down a familiar hallway. Several doors later, he arrived at a plain door with a plain plaque. The Pipes, his home away from home. At least, he hoped it still remembered him. His chest released a heavy sigh as he reached for the handle. A sharp and immediate racket assaulted his ears when he pulled the door open. It gave him pause. What once served as a warm and welcoming blanket now felt like a warning. He took a needed breath and slipped into the dark passage.

Conduits and electrical panels framed his field of vision. Recessed lighting painted sinister shadows around the interior. Roy took cautious steps as burly regulars tromped around him. He thought of calling them by name, but they still dismissed his presence. Bob, the two-ringed ringneck, wandered by without saying hello. Soiled duds clung to his slumped shoulders. A hard day's work radiated from his skin. Roy could feel the tug of respect and friendship, but it was cold and distant. Suddenly, the number of rings along his neck didn't matter in the slightest.

Bob slapped the big red button at the end of the hallway and entered the main bar. A chorus of salutations greeted his arrival. Clancy and Duncan were among them. Roy could see the pair from afar, perched on their usual stools as Fiona tended to their needs. And much to his delight, his own favorite perch was empty and waiting.

Roy smiled, but halted inside the corridor. He settled against the wall and merged with the shadows, content to relive his former life from a distance. Thirsty patrons continued to stroll by without a sliver of curiosity. They punched the big red button and joined their brethren. Reenie, another friend and talented welder, knocked the button with her favorite *ratta-tat-tatta* pattern before receiving her own chorus of welcomes.

Roy smirked and nodded.

And then someone grabbed his shoulder from behind.

Roy flinched into a spin and found Zip looming over him.

The reptilian sneered, then gestured back to the entrance.

Roy sighed and followed him outside.

The door closed behind them, muffling the ruckus. Zip hiked down the hallway a bit, enough to avoid any curious ears. He found a tolerable distance, then turned to face Roy.

"How the fuck do you stand that place?" Zip said, shaking off the experience.

Roy shrugged. "Kinda the charm. Keeps the riffraff out."

Zip narrowed his eyes, unsure of whether the insult was intentional or not. "Anyway, you've been summoned."

"Huh?" Roy checked his comdev. "I didn't receive a message."

"Not that kind of summons." Zip handed him a slip of paper.

"No coms. Power down and report to this location immediately."

Roy unfolded the paper, cocked an eyebrow, then returned his gaze to Zip. "Is this a joke?"

"Does it look like I'm laughing?"

"First of all, I'm not sure you *can* laugh. Second of all, is this a joke?"

"You have one hour. Gamon is waiting." Zip turned away and took his leave.

Roy sighed again, then turned the other way and started back to the pod station. He tossed a mournful glance at The Pipes as he passed.

* * *

Fifty-five minutes later, Roy was speed walking down a colorful corridor. His destination, an obscure education district, was fast approaching. But when he reached the end of the tunnel, his shoes squeaked to a stop. A kaleidoscopic maelstrom assaulted his senses from every direction, forcing his brain into dreamscape mode. There it was, a plenitude of pointlessness, the ultimate haven for the clinically weird and chronically bored.

He had reached the Jester District.

Once again, his pleated slacks and button shirt outed him as a trespasser. The dapper image stuck out among pink tutus, feather hats, rainbow suspenders, and layers of face paint. A small army of eager students crowded inside the junction. They all fought to justify their existence by mastering skills that nobody asked for.

Roy pulled his gaze around the hub.

Omega School of Hack-n-Sack.

Miming Made Easy.

Death Match Juggle Time.

And there, nestled in the center, was his destination: The Yuk Yuk Clown Academy.

Roy sighed, shook his head, checked his comdev, forgot he had turned it off, grunted with annoyance, searched for a wall clock, found one with abstract digits, struggled to understand it, grunted again, asked the nearest mime, realized his mistake, then gave up and leapt into a jog towards the academy.

He ducked some hacky sacks before slowing to a stop at the entrance. The exterior was modest in size, but utterly bonkers in coloration. One could spend an entire day just trying to identify a color they *didn't* use. Sinuous letters and images created a psychedelic portrait that would make a carnival blush.

Roy grabbed a bright pink handle and yanked the door open. A jarring *yuk-yuk* greeted his arrival into a small foyer. Framed images of smiling clowns covered the rainbow-striped walls. They extended onto the ceiling, giving him the distinct impression of an aerial attack. Never in his life had he felt so painfully uncomfortable.

His mortified gaze lowered to a greeting desk along the far wall. Sitting behind it was a smiling receptionist dressed in a frilly outfit. Her bulb-like head and triangular teeth filled Roy with a sense of dread, as if he had stepped into the opening scene of a horror movie. Her three large eyes blinked independently, which didn't help matters.

"Are you down to clown?" the lady said with a nasal voice.

Flee for your life! said Roy's brain. "Uuuh ..." said Roy's mouth.

A side door cracked open.

Roy held his breath and braced for a jolly murder, but then Gamon peeked around the frame. His lungs emptied at the sight, a much-needed and very welcome relief. Gamon plucked an unlit cigar from his lips and motioned for Roy to join him.

Roy maintained a stiffened posture as he shuffled towards the door.

The receptionist maintained a creepy perma-grin as she watched him slip inside.

Roy and Gamon strolled down a vibrant hallway with multicolored doors, the entrances to small theaters and classrooms. Roy could not help but wonder what horrors were trapped behind them. Gamon stopped at a blue door, surveyed the hallway, then let himself inside. Roy followed him in and the door latched behind them.

Roy glanced around an examination room, the very same that one might find in a hospital. Only in this one, everything was exaggerated to comedic proportions. Giant tongue depressors, giant reflex hammer, funhouse mirror over the sink. A smiling clown adorned the wall, holding its still-beating heart in front of a gaping chest hole. The heart itself had eyes, teeth, and looked to be having a swell time.

The clock on the wall ticked to a new hour.

Gamon grunted. "Good timing." He grabbed a chair, took a seat, and lit his cigar.

Roy, having no idea what to say or where to look, hopped onto the examination table and folded his hands like a would-be patient.

Gamon chuckled. "Relax, my friend."

Roy complied as best he could. He closed his eyes for a quick reset, then fished the slip of paper from his breast pocket. "Got your message."

"My apologies for the abrupt summons. I know you were enjoying some personal time and I regret having to cut it short."

Roy shrugged. "The nature of the biz, right?"

Gamon grinned and nodded. "I should also apologize for the location. Given the nature of the assignment, I needed somewhere inconspicuous."

"So you chose a clown school?" Roy studied the room with a slow pan, as if to track an angry bee. "This is where serial killers are *made*."

"I employ a few gophers here. It's one of the very few places that Durangoni doesn't give a shit about. In fact, I think they have two cameras for the entire district. No sane person wants to monitor clowns all day. At least, no sane person who wants to remain sane."

"Good point. So what's the job?"

Gamon plucked the cigar from his mouth and released a puff of smoke. "Werner needs to make an important delivery. He asked for you specifically."

"Me? Why?"

Gamon reached into his pocket and withdrew a subatomic

transport puck. He tossed it at Roy, who caught it with both hands. A clump of purple matter was encased in clear composite. Same weight, same feel, same rush of panic.

"He said you would be familiar with that particular cargo."

Roy's hands began to tremble, but he managed a slight nod.

"I need you to deliver that puck to a bloat house in the Kink Rinks."

"Bloat house?"

"A processing station. You're going to help them extract the contents for distribution. Werner has placed a high value on your previous experience. He wants you to oversee it."

Roy sighed and bowed his head. "So I'm a drug dealer now."

Gamon huffed and chewed his cigar. "You're in the business, Roy. What you choose to call yourself is irrelevant. The job is the job."

"I know, but—"

"But nothing. This isn't an offer."

Roy thought for a moment, then nodded.

"Good boy. You'll also need this." Gamon retrieved an activation clamp, the same kind that Werner had used on the previous puck. Silver, handheld, touchpad, everything Roy remembered. Gamon set it on the neon pink counter next to him. "The activation code is Pastry Post Deck 8 to 12. Werner said that you were a big enough nerd to know what that meant."

Roy nodded. *Pi, digits eight through twelve after the decimal*, he thought to himself.

"Good. Remember it. Don't do anything stupid like write it down."

Roy nodded.

"You are to deliver the puck to a gal named Praxie inside the Goruvian Grotto. It's an artificial cavern located inside the N2 Kink Rink. With me so far?"

"Yes sir," Roy said.

(In fact, Roy was intimately familiar with the location. The faux cavern was a must-visit for anyone with a nocturnal fetish. It housed an array of brothels in near-darkness, offering patrons everything from vampire cosplay to the infamous Mystery Hole, a pitch-black room with padded walls and an "anything goes" attitude. The only guarantees were that something would touch your junk and you wouldn't be fatally wounded. Roy had participated once in the distant past and had yet to determine whether he enjoyed the experience.)

"This is an immediate action. You will leave here and go straight there. She is expecting you by the end of the cycle."

"Yes sir."

"There's a brewpub just outside the main corridor. Sit at the bar, order a Firetooth Sandworm, and wait for someone to make contact. They will escort you to Praxie. From that point on, you're on your own. Do what they say and you'll be home before you know it. Understood?"

"Yes sir."

Gamon leaned forward and patted Roy's knee, as if to conclude the examination.

Roy half-expected a lollipop.

Gamon grunted as he rose to his feet and stretched away some soreness. The clown school chairs were a bit too small for his bulky frame (but ideal for hospital slapstick). Gamon seemed more out of place than Roy. The absence of his mobster lair proved a bit unsettling, so Roy knew the assignment carried a lot of unseen weight.

"Keep your comdev off until you reach a pod station. Use public transport and stay above the merchant line. No back channels. I will contact you for a debrief once the task is done."

"Yes sir."

"Good man," Gamon said, then exited the room.

The door latched shut, leaving Roy alone on the examination table. A cold silence infected the room, broken only by a thumping heartbeat. His troubled gaze crept over to the countertop, where the puck clamp rested in wait. Its glossy surface reflected the overhead light, taunting his mind with the exact position he never wanted to be in.

A knock at the door snatched his attention.

"Y—yes?" he said.

The door cracked open, allowing the smiling receptionist to peek her head inside. Her three eyes blinked randomly as her shark-like teeth parted. "Are you down to clown?" she said with a spine-chilling whisper.

"Nope!" Roy said as he sprung off the table and landed on the floor. "Nope!" he said as he swiped the clamp from the counter. "Nope!" he said as he pocketed the puck and hurried to the door. "Nope! Nope! Nope!" he said as he pushed into the hallway and fled the school as quickly as possible.

CHAPTER 15

Roy sat at the rear of a pod train, staring at nothing while stars in the black abyss twinkled overhead. The colossal wall of the next ring drew closer and closer, then zipped overhead as the train punched through the atmo barrier and into an express tunnel. Trips to the Kink Rinks took a while, so Roy had plenty of time alone with his thoughts.

One of his favorite travel games was guessing who would remain on board when the first Kink Rink passed overhead. Most passengers shuffled to detachment pods that broke away and vanished into the suburbs. But a few always remained. Suits and ties, sweats and sneakers, none of it mattered. Everyone had a fetish that needed attention from time to time. Roy had a few, but this time around, business would veto pleasure.

Conversations faded into the background. The puck was heavy in his pocket, like a loaded gun in search of a victim. Many times he had filled that seat, palms sweating, heart pounding with anticipation. But now it pounded with apprehension. Shame had poisoned his headspace, rendering him a silent and distant observer.

Another wall passed overhead. The train filled with a crimson glow, signaling the arrival at the first Kink Rink. The familiar transition yanked Roy out of his stupor. His gaze crept around the remaining passengers, all of which refused to make eye contact. A four-armed temptress in fishnet stockings moseyed into an adjacent car just before it detached. It was a well-practiced move from a well-practiced worker. Admirable in its own light, like a seasoned grunt on their way to a dig site.

Roy returned his gaze to the other passengers, all of whom retreated under hats and cloaks while carrying obvious stigmas. *First-timers*, he thought, then wondered what they thought of him. The Kink Rinks conjured many emotions, but dread and suspense were rarely among them. Perhaps a spousal confrontation, maybe a transactional dispute. Or, perhaps they were burdened by their own demons and didn't think of him at all. Roy had done incredible things, and yet, he remained a forgettable presence. He carried a pocket full of horror, but no one noticed. No one cared. He sighed, having realized that his life had come full circle.

The train punched through the atmo barrier of the target ring, then pinged with approaching separation. Roy maintained a sullen expression as his pod detached and curled into a side tunnel. After a few dips and dives, it slowed to a stop at the first station. The doors slid open, allowing a cloud of indulgence to invade the cabin. Flashing neon, howls of boozy laughter, and of course, the salty stench of lustful abandon. A group of loud-mouthed tourists stomped into the cabin and claimed some open seats. The doors slid shut and the pod whisked towards the next stop.

Roy cringed at his new travel mates.

And then he felt guilty for cringing.

He knew those people.

He *was* those people.

For everyone numbs the pain of existence.

Several stops later, Roy excused himself from a mass of drunken hoodlums and exited the pod into a sensual assault. The sector was ablaze with activity. Bright hologram ads littered the walls, cycling through seductive images. Black floors concealed numerous stains and rubbish. Cleaner bots hummed along as they struggled to sanitize an ever-tainted landscape. The crowd churned with all shapes and sizes, all races and sexes, all creeds and classes, pulsing as a stark contrast to the hygienic central rings.

Roy patted the puck inside his pocket. Still there, still heavy, still pulling him towards an unwanted appellation. He took a needed breath, then straightened his shirt and began the long trek to the Goruvian Grotto.

The Kink Rinks, while well-known for their boundless debaucheries, were not known for logical interiors. Their avenues twisted and turned over one another, creating an endless maze that confused and disoriented visitors. This was by design, as lost patrons tend to spend more credits. In fact, the deeper one ventured, the more delectable the reward. The most salacious brothels were also the hardest to find. The idea was, once you got there, it took an act of pure heroic will to leave.

As such, regulars to the Kink Rinks got really good at getting around. This wasn't a kooky sense of pride, but more of an outright necessity. "Got lost while getting bent" was not an excuse that employers were willing to accept.

Roy knew this well.

Roy also knew how to find the Goruvian Grotto.

Like a dog on a homeward journey, Roy followed his mental nose up ramps, down stairs, around bends, and over bridges. The very notion of "levels" was notably absent inside the ring. The interior seemed to twist and curl over itself, forming a giant metal pretzel without cessation. Its design was either an architectural wonder or a hideous drunken accident, a debate that often reared its head inside its many pubs and diners. Nevertheless, it remained a glorious destination for anyone with an itch to scratch.

Roy's usual grin and forward stare had morphed into vigilance. His reduced pace allowed him to absorb sights that he had once ignored. He met eyes with grifters and hucksters trying to fund their next fix. Their ratty clothes and bloodshot stares conjured waves of pity, something previously dismissed as background noise. He peeked inside dark alleys where groups of addicts traded pills and needles.

Their frail bodies leaned against filthy walls and dumpsters. The ablest among them scrounged for scraps in an effort to see the next day. The perennial musk, once seen as the peak of leisure, had revealed itself as soiled desperation.

The puck grew heavier in his pocket.

Hologram signs flashed from every direction. Neon letters and blinking arrows promised great times at affordable prices. Jezebels from all walks of life winked at Roy through cloudy windows. Red hues dominated the space, consuming the cooler hues of pubs and grub. Every hovel barked its own version of thumping music, serving as a constant buffer between the barfs and cackles. Every so often, a mystery stain would grip the sole of his shoe, prompting a cringe that his mind quickly snuffed away.

Roy crested a small hill to reveal his destination, a churning hollow known as the Goruvian Grotto. It spanned an area the size of a football field and rose several stories into the putrid air. Countless stairwells connected the base to the upper levels, all of which were open-faced and flashing neon adverts. A tangled web of pipes and ducts snaked across the ceiling, giving the chamber a cold industrial vibe.

One wall, however, was a towering void of darkness. No light, no levels, just a looming gateway to a nocturnal realm. It housed a bordello of black where dreams came true under a shroud of darkness. Patrons wandered to and from the chasm, wearing an array of interesting expressions. Most eager, some frightened, others exhausted as they returned to the light. Roy watched as battered bodies emerged from the portal, only to vanish into the core ruckus, like wounded soldiers returning from battle.

The roar of activity was impossible to ignore. Peddlers shouted from the upper decks while the base slithered with constant motion. Mobile shacks littered the arena, resembling a derelict shantytown. The hustle and bustle of roving commerce defined the space, offering everything from erotic toys to illicit encounters. A handful of permanent structures rose above the shacks, one of which was The Brink, a popular pub that rested at the portal base.

Roy's destination.

A hologram logo flashed above it, showcasing its namesake in wavy blue letters. The pub served as a makeshift lighthouse, offering a final shot of courage before crossing into the great unknown. Stories brimmed within its walls, many of which Roy had planted himself. The logo blinked and rotated, as if to wave him over for another round. Roy smirked, but the nostalgia would be short-lived. He restored his grimace and proceeded down the hill.

Cackles and shoulder bumps greeted his arrival at the shanties. Nothing personal, just a general neglect of couth and self-awareness. Groups of friends gathered around rickety sheds filled with skimpy hustlers. Creepy loners gawked at the latest sexbots. Paper fliers littered the ground, each stamped with erotic pics and detailed maps. Roy maneuvered through the madness, trying his best to avoid unwanted confrontations.

Given the near-constant intoxication, petty squabbles were a common sight within the Kink Rinks. Durangoni Security maintained an unseen presence to protect the workers. They quashed any scuffle that got out of hand, but largely ignored anything below a stabbing. Roy took pride in his willingness to throw a punch, but only now did he understand the power of restraint. Anyone could stand their ground, but true composure was tested in the shadows.

A few knocks and stumbles later, Roy found himself standing outside The Brink. Its stony exterior lifted from the ground like a mighty castle, despite being a two-story box with barred windows. His gaze climbed up the craggy facade and settled on the bright blue letters rotating overhead. A knot formed inside his stomach and crawled into his throat. He stepped towards the door, which swung open and slammed into the wall, compliments of a drunken brute on his way to an epic bender. Barks and clatters spilled from within, but faded into the background rumble. Roy took the opportunity to slip inside without touching the grimy handle.

A thick cloud of funk welcomed him into a foyer with sullied walls and a rugged floor. Roy cringed as a mixture of booze, barf, and breadsticks assaulted his nostrils. The pub was half-full, but sounded near-capacity. Social norms did not apply, so customers howled their every thought without a hint of shame. No one noticed his presence, not even the leggy hostess who wandered by and glanced over his head.

Roy was an unseen apparition.

Unassuming, unattractive, uninteresting, un-everything.

Gamon's favorite gopher.

He sighed, bowed his head, and shuffled towards the bar.

The bartender, a stout cyclops with a scruffy beard and rumpled hide, clunked several mugs of grog onto the counter and slid them towards a group of waiting dude-bros. Grunts of gratitude responded. They raised their mugs, toasted to their lechery, and erupted in hurrahs before dispersing. The barman watched with a blank expression, but then a squeaky stool hooked his attention. He turned to find a sheepish Roy occupying the seat.

The cyclops sneered and cocked his brow, dive-bar speak for *Whaddaya want?*

"Firetooth Sandworm, please," Roy said.

The cyclops stared him down, then turned away and plucked some bottles from the rear shelves. Roy watched intently as the barkeep poured and shook a multi-sauce concoction. He dumped the elixir into a highball glass, then struck a match and dropped it into the liquid, stem and all. The drink flared to life and shot a fiery column into the air that lasted far too long. Roy swallowed his alarm as the flame died to a flicker. The cyclops knocked the drink towards him, spilling a dab of flaming booze onto the counter before turning to the next customer.

Roy studied the still-burning liquid, unsure of how he was supposed to drink it. A hearty blow failed to extinguish the flame. It just flickered back to life and taunted him like a trick candle on a birthday cake. A stronger blow failed again, prompting a grunt and eye roll. He sighed with annoyance, then turned to find a giant bloodshot eyeball staring at him from the adjacent stool. Roy yelped into a near-tumble, but broke his fall with a hasty counter grab.

"Fuckin' hell," he said with a death grip on the bar. He closed his eyes for a quick reset, then returned his gaze to the creature.

A sheet of milky skin encased the head-sized orb. It was attached to a rigid stalk that snaked around the stool and down to the floor. At knee-level, the serpentine body split into four legs that tucked into leather boots. Roy traced the body back to the giant eye, which continued to glare at him through a deep brown iris. The skin sheet crawled around the orb and came together with a wet snap, which Roy could only assume was a blink.

"Can I, um ... help you?" Roy said, firmly recoiled.

"Who sent you?" the eyeball said from a well-hidden mouth.

"Gamon." Roy craned his neck to try and find the orifice. "Here to meet Praxie."

"Got the product?"

"Yes." Roy gestured down to his lap. He reached into his pocket and withdrew the puck, keeping it hidden inside his palm.

The eyeball rotated downward, wet-blinked, then rotated back. "Follow me," it said, then unraveled from the stool and waddled towards the exit.

Roy glanced at his still-flaming shot. The bartender wandered by, snuffed the flame with his beefy palm, then tossed it down his own gullet, all without making eye contact. Roy glared at the brute, then realized he hadn't paid. *Fair enough*, he thought to himself, then hopped off the stool and jogged to catch up with the walking eye-stalk.

CHAPTER 16

The eyestalk toddled to the front door and bumped it open with its noodly body, exiting The Brink. Roy followed it outside into the roaring grotto. Several necks turned to ogle the creature, a jarring sight even in the Kink Rinks. It had learned to ignore the stares, which saddened Roy and conjured some long-forgotten empathy. They strolled through the underworld as polar opposites of the visual spectrum. One unseeable. One unsettling.

The creature moseyed around the pub and towards the giant black hole behind it. *Of course it likes the dark*, Roy thought, then immediately felt guilty for thinking it. *I am such a dickhole*, he thought in response, hoping to balance out the karma.

They walked up a short incline and passed through the cavern entrance. An unseen barrier killed the grotto lights and banished the roar into the distant background. The sudden darkness stopped Roy in his tracks, forcing a search for visual bearings. As his eyes adjusted, faint blue lines began to reveal themselves. They defined edges and outlined objects, including himself. The holo-trace system allowed visitors to see without ruining the nocturnal experience. Bright enough to avoid obstacles, dim enough to remain anonymous.

Roy glanced around the multi-story cavern. Numerous stairs and ramps led to a myriad of doors and hallways, all of them outlined for convenience. Patrons of all persuasions wandered through the murky maze, hunting for their erotic encounters. An unspoken gag rule rendered the place eerily silent. Heel clacks echoed like jackhammers. Door whines cut through the space like ghostly howls. Roy traced a winding stairwell down to the floor, where the outline of a wobbling eyestalk shrunk with every step.

Roy jogged to catch up.

He followed the creature around a bend and into a hidden hallway. The silence deepened, amplifying their footsteps. They passed the outlines of unmarked doors, each housing a distant ruckus. The eyestalk waddled to a stop at the end of the passage. It double-checked for its Roy companion, then gazed into a hidden panel. A soft ping confirmed the iris scan, prompting an unseen door to slide open. Roy followed the beast into an ebon box. The door slid shut and the floor began its slow descent.

The interior lights flickered on, quelling the darkness. Roy winced at the sudden brightness and blinked to readjust. The elevator car was remarkably clean. Pristine, even. Each wall was a spotless plane of smooth metal. Panels on the floor and ceiling glowed with a frosty hue. A dull hum of descent served as a backdrop to the awkward silence.

"So, um ..." Roy said. "What's your name?"

The creature maintained its forward stare.

"I'm Roy."

The creature wet-blinked, then twisted its giant eye to Roy. "Lenny," it said from a yet-to-be-seen mouth.

"Nice to meet you, Lenny."

Lenny's eye flaps puckered a bit, which Roy could only assume was a smile.

The floor pushed on their heels as the elevator slowed to a stop. The door slid open to reveal a large factory bustling with activity. Roy and Lenny emerged onto a catwalk that encircled the plant. Guards in black uniforms clomped along the grated metal, eyeing the work floor beneath them. Numerous stations littered the arena, housing countless peons that assembled nodes and passed them along. Conveyor belts slithered through the workspace, shuttling parts throughout the factory. Chains and tethers dangled from the ceiling like moss from a mighty tree.

An odd place for a drug distributor.

Or perhaps, the ideal cover for one.

Resting at the center was a large dome with a row of port windows. Conveyor belts ran from it, but not to it. A small regiment of guards patrolled the perimeter. Roy leaned on the railing and studied the structure from afar. Not a foreman office, that much was certain.

"Come," Lenny said as he started down a stairwell.

Roy followed him down to the work floor, then along a marked path towards the center. The workers ignored them, content to toil away at their stations. They all wore the same white aprons and green gloves. A painful sterility infected the air. Unseen chemicals floated through the space, stinging lungs with every inhale.

A guard snickered and shook his head as Lenny waddled by. Roy glared at the guard as he passed, which the guard saw fit to return. Lenny continued his trek up to a small group chatting beside the dome. He slowed to a stop and stared at the nearest member, a suited brute with gray skin and numerous warts.

Lenny cleared his throat.

The brute glanced at the eyestalk and huffed. "The cock-eye is back."

The rest of the group chuckled.

Roy, heeding the need to maintain civility, decided to stay quiet. "Ass-wart fucker says what?" he said with an assertive tone.

"What?" the brute said.

The group chuckled even louder.

Lenny puckered his flaps in response.

The brute turned to Roy and puffed his chest. "Care to say that again?"

Roy, always one to diffuse a strained situation, contemplated a heartfelt apology. "Ass," he said, then took a step forward. "Wart." Another step. "Fucker." A final step brought them face to face. "Says what?"

The brute snarled, but the confrontation was cut short.

"That's enough," said a scratchy female voice.

The group parted to reveal a dark-haired vixen leaning against the dome wall. Her leathery garb looked better suited for a mercenary ship than a factory floor. She sprang off the wall and sauntered towards Roy, unveiling her violet eyes and ashy face. Her wiry frame looked brittle in a way, despite her bold and confident stride. Her boots clacked to a rest, cueing a hard lean and chin cock. She looked Roy up and down, then smirked.

"Piss off, Klurp," she said to the brute without making eye contact. "And take your band of fuckwits with you."

The brute nodded, then slunk away with his posse in tow. He tossed a glare at Roy before turning down the entry path.

The woman crossed her arms and grunted. "So you're the guy, eh?"

"I'm a guy," Roy said with an affable tone. "Can't say if I'm *the* guy."

"Gamon sent you, no?"

"Ah, yes. That guy I am." He extended a hand. "Roy."

"Praxie," she said and completed the shake. "Been waiting for you."

"Am I late?"

"No. Been waiting all the same." She glanced at the eyestalk. "That'll be all, Lenny."

Lenny wet-blinked, then turned away and headed back to the stairs.

"Hey Lenny," Roy said.

The eyestalk paused and twisted back to Roy.

"Thanks for the escort. I appreciate it."

Lenny pucker-smiled, then untwisted and resumed his trek.

"Good guy, that one," Roy said to Praxie. "Got a question, though."

"What the hell is he?"

"Yes, please."

Praxie shrugged. "No one knows. Lenny never talks about his past and there are no other species like him on the station. Trust me, I've looked. Mutant would be my best guess. Maybe a botched experiment. I strongly suspect that he escaped a bad situation. Landed here a while back, been working the grotto ever since."

They watched from afar as Lenny climbed the stairs, albeit awkwardly.

"And you're right," she said with a tender tone. "He is a good guy."

She spun around and plodded in the opposite direction, making her way around the dome. Her long gait forced Roy into a light jog to keep up. He eyed the port windows along the wall, which glowed bright enough to conceal the interior. Praxie thumped her shoulder into a sturdy entry door. The pane swung open and they proceeded inside.

Roy squinted as a golden glare consumed them. Praxie sauntered towards the center of a large round room. Roy glanced around the edgeless space, resembling the interior of a giant metal donut. A continuous lighting strip glowed above the port windows. Every square inch sloped down to a focal point. Roy peeked around Praxie to find a mounting rod rising from the axis. He frowned, recalling the same setup from the Sunken Isles. The dome was an extraction bowl, just on a much smaller scale.

Praxie's heels clacked to a halt beside the mount. She turned to Roy and swung an open hand over the rod, as if to present a prize. "I trust you know what to do?"

"Y—yes," Roy said with a reluctant tone.

A brief silence settled between them.

Praxie sighed, then rolled her wrist, gesturing to *get on with it*.

"Ah, yes, sorry." Roy fished the puck and clamp from his pockets. Beads of sweat rolled down his face as he joined them together. The claws snapped around the puck and the device powered on, ready to receive command. *Pastry Post Deck 8 to 12*, he thought. *Pi, digits eight through twelve after the decimal. 3.1415926 ... 53589.* His heart raced as he repeated the code. *53589 ... 53589 ... 53589.*

"Is something wrong?" Praxie said with a hint of annoyance.

"No, s'all good."

He pressed five.

Praxie narrowed her gaze.

"It's just ..."

He pressed three.

Praxie cocked her neck.

"I just, um ..."

He pressed five.

And then everything stopped.

Roy froze in realization.

Praxie froze in confusion.

He met her gaze, then slowly shook his head. "I can't do this," he said with a meager voice, then spun and sprinted for the door.

Praxie's confusion snapped into anger. "What the f—stop!" Her words echoed through the chamber as Roy crashed through the door. She gave chase and slid to a halt outside the dome. Her widened gaze whipped around the factory and locked onto Roy sprinting for the exit. She pointed and screamed. "Stop him!"

All activity came to an abrupt stop, save for Roy's galloping retreat. Every worker turned to the commotion, but did not bother to get involved. Every guard zeroed in on Roy. Some chased him down the gangway while others leapt from the catwalk to cut off the stairs, barring the path to and from. Roy skidded to a halt and looked to his sides, only to see guards closing in from the factory floor.

He was trapped.

Panic ensued.

The guards inched towards him from every direction. Stun batons crackled in their hands, cutting through a hanging tension. Workers continued to watch with mild interest as the guards surrounded their target. Roy spun around with the puck in hand, searching for outs that no longer existed. He whimpered as a gruesome fate engulfed him.

The clacks of Praxie's heels echoed from afar. She sauntered down the gangway, cold and confident in her approach. A callous smirk crept across her face. She would savor the torture, as she always did.

But then a guard screamed.

And another.

They all staggered backwards, then turned and fled.

Praxie watched a frightened guard tumble over a workstation, then keep going. Her puzzled gaze returned to the gangway where a frothing beast occupied the space. Its hunched back and clouded eyes drew an immediate flinch and backtrack. It snarled at her as an acidic brew spilled from its mouth.

A tense standoff commenced.

The workers held their breath.

But not for long, as they too would scream and flee when the beast shrieked and gave chase to the vixen. Praxie matched the shriek and spun into her own sprint. She rounded the dome with flailing arms and disappeared. Roy skidded to a halt and about-faced. Using the chaos as cover, he resumed his sprint towards the elevator.

Another guard burst through a perimeter door with a spear-like weapon in hand. It crackled with captive charge. He aimed it at a fleeing Roy and pulled the trigger, releasing a violent blast of energy. The bolt whizzed over his shoulder and destroyed a nearby workstation. Roy yelped, but maintained his stride.

Another bolt.

Another miss.

Another yelp.

Roy sailed around some heavy machinery and into the stairwell, shielding him from aim. The guard sprinted down the catwalk to reset. Roy had precious few seconds to summon the lift. He darted up the stairs, across the catwalk, and slapped the control panel. The elevator dinged, but the car wasn't there. It began a slow descent from above, content to milk additional stress from the situation. Roy groaned with frustration, but there was nothing to do. He could only hope that the car arrived before the next blast ripped him to shreds.

The guard's clanking sprint grew louder and louder.

Roy cringed and slapped the panel eight more times.

The clanks grew louder, and louder, and stopped.

A sudden thump and clatter cued an array of curses.

Roy peeked around a pillar to see the guard sprawled over the catwalk. He had tripped and fallen, sending his weapon tumbling down to the factory floor. The guard barked with pain and scrambled to right the mishap. Lenny stood behind him, watching the ruckus while trying to look innocent. He met gazes with Roy and pucker-smiled.

Roy returned the smile and nodded.

The elevator dinged.

* * *

It should come as no surprise that Roy escaped. He rode the elevator back to the grotto, sprinted to the cavern mouth, and vanished into the crowd. And when I say *vanished*, I mean exactly that. He slipped into the mass and disappeared. I studied hours of footage, tracing his every step until he turned the proverbial corner.

Poof.

Gone.

No trace whatsoever.

To this day, I have no idea how Roy fled the Rinks. But given where he ended up, the only thing I knew for certain was that he had some help. How? Because two weeks later, Praxie and her goons found him inside the core.

But we'll get to that.

I just wanted to know how he got there.

I staked out the Goruvian Grotto for several days, hoping to uncover pieces of the puzzle. Drunken dregs were more than happy to muse on Roy's antics, which, apparently, was all the buzz in the underworld. None were helpful, but all were entertaining. I even chatted with a few of the factory workers, all of whom declined to be interviewed.

The mystery persisted.

And then, late on the third day, while sipping on my fourth Firetooth Sandworm inside The Brink, I saw an eyestalk creature waddle through the front door.

I greeted Lenny and coaxed him into a friendly conversation. He carried no veneer or pretense, which was disarming at first. I got the distinct impression that he was just happy to be needed. He and Roy were much alike in that way. I enjoyed my chat with Lenny, despite his dry demeanor and penchant for using the least amount of words to make his point. Our meeting was short and sweet, as Lenny was unable (or perhaps unwilling) to add any tantalizing details. Below is a brief excerpt.

Did you help Roy escape the factory by tripping the guard?

Roy was a kind person. I consider him a friend.

And did he give you any indication of where he was going?

Roy was a kind person. I consider him a friend.

I can't tell if you're being candid or avoidant.

Roy was a kind person. I consider him a friend.

Did you, um ... was Roy a kind person and do you consider him a friend?

(wet-blinks) Yes.

CHAPTER 17

Two weeks after his miraculous escape, Roy was found in the core of Durangoni. This fact alone was itself miraculous, as core folk did not suffer the peons. Roy had earned a respectable income working as Gamon's lackey, but his bank account was nowhere near the capacity it took to fraternize with engineering royalty. Coupled with a security system that rivaled nuclear silos, it made his presence ever so mysterious.

Thus, he needed help.

And given his connection to a particular dissident, one could surmise where it came from. (Vierra Belliosa has never confirmed her involvement and my journalistic integrity prevents me from implicating her. But, c'mon.)

In any regard, Roy was hiding in the core. Someone saw him and reported the breach, which was likely intercepted by Werner and relayed to Praxie. Let us not forget that Roy was carrying a fortune's worth of Snake Bone on his person. He betrayed Gamon, which blacklisted him in the trafficking network. He betrayed Werner, which likely placed him on Zip's "special friends" list. Roy was now the most wanted being in the quadrant. His world had utterly imploded, all thanks to a pesky rush of conscience.

The stage was set for a messy confrontation.

* * *

Roy had always wanted to see the core, just not as a desperate fugitive. He lay on the rooftop of a luxury mart that catered to the obscenely rich. Any single item cost more than he could ever make as a plumber. The store's dumpster carried more value than a mid-level merchant shop, a fact that was not lost on him whenever he plundered it for morsels. After all, a hunted criminal beggar could not be a chooser.

Roy munched on a half-eaten sandwich while gazing into a giant sky lake.

Yes, a giant lake in the sky.

To understand the core of Durangoni, one must first understand centrifugal force. There is no *weight* at the core of a planet because there is no *down*. Force is equal from all directions, which neutralizes gravity. Durangoni was no different, so any normalized weight needed to be created. The core was a long cylinder from pole to pole, serving as a hub for the ring system. Its hollow interior was five miles in diameter with crisscrossing beams that supported the structure. The core rotated independently, creating enough gravity to keep everything glued to the walls. Thus, when Roy gazed into the sky, he gazed at the other side of a rotating barrel.

A barrel, in this case, populated by eggheads and the uber-wealthy.

The lake in Roy's sky was constructed for an energy mogul who loved to fish. His personal mega-yacht floated on his personal lake while his personal staff processed the exotic fish that he had personally selected for his personal lake. All inside the core of Durangoni, one of the most expensive pieces of real estate in the known universe. The sheer magnitude of opulence was difficult to comprehend. So stunning was the lake's impracticality that Roy could waste hours dissecting the physics of its creation.

His gaze wandered the vast enclosure, a round horizon filled with nerve centers and lavish mansions. Maglev rails shuttled the rich and nerdy around the interior. Personal vehicles were strictly prohibited, as drunken accidents could disable critical systems. Given the core's vital role in the survival of a trillion beings, security was paramount. It took extraordinary levels of power and influence to gain access, a reality that plagued Roy with constant anxiety. His presence was an extreme anomaly, one that carried an equally extreme punishment.

Nevertheless, he was stuck there.

But all the same, it was better than anywhere else.

And so he waited.

Two weeks he had called that rooftop home. Two weeks of sleeping on a hard surface with artificial sunlight battering his eyelids. For once, he actually missed his ratty cot in the sub-core. Roy was surrounded by an ostentatious landscape, a life he had coveted from his first day aboard the station. And yet, in that lowest of moments, he would have given anything to slumber in the bowels of anonymity.

And then a faint squeak caught his attention.

Roy sat up and raked his gaze across the rooftop. The vents were quiet. No wind or chatting locals. Another faint squeak snapped his gaze to a nearby access ladder. A sudden terror swelled inside his chest. He scrambled to his feet and tiptoed to a hidden corner for a covert peek. When he peered over the ledge, his gut seized with panic. Praxie stood in the back alley. She monitored a pair of burly goons who were climbing the ladder as quietly as they could.

Roy swallowed a gasp and stumbled backwards. With precious little time, he spun around and sprinted towards a small satchel resting in the opposite corner. His loud clops prompted the goons to bark with urgency and hurry up the ladder. Roy skidded to a halt, snatched the satchel, and slung it over his shoulder as the first goon poked his head above the roofline. They met eyes for a split second, contrasting their fear and focus.

Roy leapt over the ledge.

It was a well-rehearsed move. That is, inside his head. Roy crashed onto a pallet of stock, which looked much softer than it actually was. The impact buckled his legs, knocked the wind from his lungs, and sent him tumbling to the ground. He wheezed in pain as distant yells gave way to canters of pursuit. No broken bones, thank goodness, but plenty of nasty knocks and soon-to-be bruises. Roy struggled to his feet and stumbled into a run.

Plan B was officially in play.

Roy emerged from the alley and onto the sidewalk, where several well-to-dos gawked at his presence. A dirty poor on *their* pristine walkway? Surely not, kind sir. Roy fled the disapproval and sprinted in the other direction. A dainty lady screamed and shooed him away, as if to shame a rat back to the sewer. The ruckus alerted the goons, who emerged from the alley as Roy ducked into another. They gritted their teeth and continued the pursuit with Praxie in tow.

Several turns later, Roy stalled outside of a processing depot. Supply drones floated around the area, tending to open bays full of lavish goods. Even they were grime-free and shining in the artificial sunlight. It was as if dirt itself had been outlawed. Roy spun around the yard in search of an exit. Security barriers blocked the bays, so he settled for a stack of crates. Not the most ideal of hiding places, but good enough for a breather. The goons grumbled nearby, then faded into the distance, having taken a wrong turn.

With time now a luxury, Roy decided to enact the next phase of his plan. He fished the comdev from his pocket, checked the clock, then placed a hasty call. "It's me," he said. "I'm pinched. Green light for the nine-block." He peeked around the crates and stared at the depot entrance. "Yes, zero the rest." The call ended. A quick swipe opened a pre-programmed screen with a flashing banner. It awaited some final input, which Roy provided. He took a deep breath, submitted the form, then returned the comdev to his pocket.

A sharp chirp startled him into a flinch. He spun around to find a supply drone staring him down with discontent. Its single red eye glanced at the crate stack, then back to him, then back to the stack, then back to him.

"Oh, sorry," Roy said, then stepped aside.

The drone floated to the stack, grabbed the top crate, then

chirped at Roy again before hovering away.

Roy sighed.

Even the robots gave him shit.

As he watched the drone rejoin its tidy brethren, his gaze fell to a porthole cover near the center of the yard. A half-grin lifted his cheek, which quickly inverted when he noticed Praxie enter the depot. He yelped and sprinted to the port. Praxie shouted for the goon squad as Roy gripped the latch handles and yanked it open, unveiling a dank sewer system (which, of course, smelled like lavender). Roy dropped through the hole and splash-landed into a river of muck, a depressingly familiar sensation. He picked a direction and fled.

Plan C, then.

The echoes of Praxie and her posse bounded through the dark tunnels. Roy huffed and puffed as his feet splashed through a thin layer of filth. Dome lights whipped overhead, reminiscent of the pod train expressway. He had no idea where he was going, but felt an urgent need to get there as quickly as possible. Blind instinct yanked him into side tunnels, hoping to delve deep enough to regain some isolation. He ducked into a random alcove and stopped dead in his tracks, letting the silence consume him.

Praxie's voice grew louder, then quieter, then vanished.

The splashes of her goons disappeared.

Roy swallowed a whimper.

The hunt was on.

Sensing the end of his psychotic adventure, Roy retrieved the puck and clamp from his satchel. He joined them together with a soft push, which powered the display. *If this is the end*, he thought, *might as well be memorable*. He sighed, then entered 5-3-5-8-9. The device pinged and unlocked the extraction protocol. He swiped the meter up to full capacity, topping out at 93 billion units. He then set a 30-second delay, just in case. After several "Are you sure?" checks, a large button turned red.

At that moment, a single tap separated Roy from a spectacular departure.

"Roy!" Praxie said, her voice echoing from an adjacent tunnel.

"You cannot escape this. All we want is the product. Hand it over and we will let you go."

Roy rolled his eyes. Even under the circumstances, he could not help but balk at such an obvious lie. "Can I get a hug too?" he said.

After an awkward silence, "Yes" echoed in response.

Roy shook his head, then emerged from the alcove and tiptoed down the tunnel. The constant trickle of water masked any obvious footsteps. His slow and steady vigilance guided him through a maze of passages, hoping for an exit. Before long, a dull and distant roar caught his attention. He crept towards the sound, using it as an audible shield. A faint glow appeared in his peripheral, stealing his focus. Sunlight. He grunted with relief and leapt into a light jog. Roy turned a final corner and slowed to a stop at the mouth of a giant egress.

The sweet relief turned sour.

Roy pulled his gaze across a massive basin of waterfalls. Countless drainpipes emptied their contents into a reservoir far below. The constant churn created a colossal whirlpool, certain death for anyone stupid enough to take the plunge. Roy groaned at the dead end and turned back to the sewer maze, only to find the smirking faces of Praxie and her goons.

"End of the line," she said.

Roy stood motionless.

She extended an open palm. "We can do this the easy way or the hard way. Your choice."

"Do I still get that hug?" Roy said in a mocking tone.

Praxie smirked and motioned to the goons, who stepped forward.

Roy lifted the clamp overhead, revealing the glowing red button.

The goons halted.

Praxie's smirk disappeared. "Wha—what are you doing?"

The smirk had reappeared on Roy's face. "Plan D it is," he said, then pressed the button and hurled the device over the ledge. It fell through the churning mist and vanished into the reservoir below. Roy expected an immediate tackle, but it never came. He turned back to Praxie and her goons, all of whom were frozen in horror. The image caught him off-guard, shifting his dismay to curiosity. "What?" he said, which cued a thundering explosion.

The violent expansion lifted the entire lake over the basin. A massive spout of filthy water surged into the sky and rained across the landscape. The entire region shook under a sudden and savage earthquake. Walls cracked. Metal screamed. Every drain flooded with backwash. Roy and his pursuers were snatched from their feet and carried through the sewer maze. Chaos consumed the valley as a raging tsunami swallowed it whole.

* * *

And thus began The Incident.

Praxie and her goons had donned faces of horror, but not for the reasons one might expect. While the loss of product was unfortunate, they were privy to two critical pieces of information that Roy was not.

First, the lake was a catch basin for Durangoni's water treatment system. Whatever dropped inside was filtered and recirculated. The orbs of Snake Bone, while a costly and disruptive clog, would have been caught and removed.

That is, if not for the second piece of information.

There were no orbs.

This particular batch was in caplet form. *Dissolvable* caplet form. Roy, unbeknownst to him, had dosed the entire space station with 93 billion units of a hallucinogenic nightmare.

A trillion beings called Durangoni home, and every one of them tripped balls for an entire week. The dilution lessened the severity, but the tainted circulation ensured a long and steady experience. With no way to combat the contamination, and with no one lucid enough to think of an alternate recourse, the entire population was forced to endure the chaos.

This period of mass psychosis, infamously dubbed The Incident, brought the station to its proverbial knees. Imagine, if you will, the single greatest assembly of creeds and cultures losing its collective grip on reality.

All at once.

For an entire week.

With no reticence or rule of law.

The disruption was, to put it gently, immeasurably disgracious. And while I would never presume to recap someone else's torment, I can reach into my own dark chasm of experience and withdraw some poignant anecdotes. The following is a candid recount of my dance with the rainbow devil.

* * *

Day One

It started as any other.

I awoke inside my condo with a mind for breakfast. After a hot shower and some extensive primping, I perused a collection of designer suits and selected a pleasing ensemble that captured the appropriate mood. I had an important meeting that day, so I landed on ashen pinstripes with a turquoise tie. Dignity with a dash of flair. Puki Horpocket always departs his master suite as a painted portrait. This day was no different and I looked positively smashing.

Too bad it was all for naught.

I strolled through a vibrant living room dripping with class and kudos. Paintings, sculptures, and of course, multiple glass cabinets filled with awards, plaques, and medals. I have no choice but to bathe in my own merit before entering the kitchen. A bit smug perhaps, but I enjoy the daily boost and prefer it to a moist toilette. I see it as a final tease and tickle before moving on to phase two of my morning routine.

I flowed into my kitchen, an austere environment with white cabinets, sharp angles, and polished metal fixtures. A gracious host I am not, as my social obligations are always met in public. Thus, my kitchen and I share a bond of severity. The coffee machine had sensed my presence and started brewing a delectable concoction that shall remain nameless. A heavenly aroma filled the space. But alas, the machine had betrayed me. It had drunk from the tainted pipes of Roy's misadventure.

This would be my first dose of Snake Bone.

A hologram panel had appeared on the adjacent wall and opened a curator view for the Definitive Directory of Durangoni. My coffee intake involves scanning the directory for any updates that required my immediate attention. The auto-rito spit out a warm breakfast wrap, which I plucked from the tray and carried over to a comfy nook. I took a seat at a small bench and table, perfect for sipping and nibbling while getting a jumpstart on the day.

And so I sipped and nibbled.

That is, until the letters started to move.

Not by much, just enough to assume that the holo-feed was glitching. I adjusted the settings as best I could, but nothing I did seemed to fix the problem. And then a capital F ate a lowercase A. Not deleted, *ate*. I can still hear the crunching and howls of agony. The graphic barbarity sparked an alphabetic panic. Entire words leapt off the screen and fell to the floor, where they flopped like fish out of water. And then the serifs declared war. A vicious battle erupted inside the directory. Uppercase Ts plunged their daggers into the soft bellies of vowels. Xs spun like buzz saws and chewed through helpless adverbs. The shrieks haunt me to this day.

I killed the feed with a stern command, which instantly wiped the battlefield. Calm returned to the kitchen, unwinding an unexpected tension. *What a tasteless prank*, I thought while sipping a second mug of nightmare fuel.

I downed a final swig and set the mug on the counter, at which point it decided to sprout several legs and skitter across the surface like a porcelain spider. I yelped and jerked backwards, as one tends to do when drinkware comes to life. The handle split into a pair of mandibles, which the spider mug gleefully used to scare the dickens out of me. Sharp tinks needled the room as the creature tapped across the counter and chomped its handle. It tried to scale a cabinet wall, but lost its grip and fell to the floor. The mug shattered into several pieces, all of which sprouted their own spider legs and skittered away.

I paused to gather my bearings while trying to ignore the swamp beast playing sad ukulele music in the corner. His name was Finkle, by the way. I know this because he waved and said, "I'm Finkle," before popping out one of his eyes, tossing it into the sink, and returning to his sad ukulele music. Bright yellow pus oozed from the socket and trickled down his chest, not that he seemed to mind. The eye in the sink began to multiply with wet pops, creating a small army of squirming orbs that cheered whenever a song ended.

Alas, my bearings would remain ungathered.

Not that it mattered much, as a legion of flaming mupmups (read: tiny hairless hyenas with a penchant for ankle biting) fell through a doom portal and galloped through the condo. Purple flames poured from their bodies, igniting everything they touched. I yelped again and raced towards the front door, which was also a pancake. Having no idea how to unlock a pancake, I crashed into the pane with a stiff shoulder, which ripped it off the hinges and launched me out into the open. Several mupmups chased me outside, but paused to devour the pancake door, all while setting the entire neighborhood on fire.

Speaking of the neighborhood, that's when things got interesting.

My community enjoyed a quiet location tucked away from the hustle and bustle of station life. As such, the enormity of the situation had been somewhat stymied. The front door of my condo opened into a rounded basin with a central garden. I shared the space with two dozen neighbors, many of whom were oblivious to the mupmup flames consuming the area. I did my best to call attention to the danger, but they seemed a bit preoccupied with their own hellscapes. One of them sprinted around the basin while swinging a lamp with homicidal intent. Another saw fit to dance naked in the garden while hissing at anyone who came near. It became abundantly clear that fleeing was the best course of action.

And so I did.

I hurried down an access hall and into another basin, which was guarded by a three-pronged unicorn named Francis. I know this because he said, "Begone, interloper! For ye have entered the blessed kingdom of Francis the Wonder Pickle!" I had questions, but I did not stick around to ask them.

After scampering through more halls and gardens, I emerged into a large pedestrian tunnel. Sorry, what I meant to say was, I emerged into a swirling vortex of pure pandemonium. It was hard to find someone who wasn't screaming. A mass of terrified citizens barked and flailed as they fought whatever torment their minds had conjured up. The one I remember the most was a small child pointing at the ceiling while grinning like a serial killer. She clutched a cabbage in the other hand, which she used to intimidate the vision.

And so I fled again, this time towards a nearby pod station.

A fresh wave of madness hit my brain as I skidded to a halt at the crowded junction. The gathered mass pulsed and twitched, as if possessed by a horde of demons. When the writhing stopped, they had all transformed into my mother. The horror. *Release me from the burden of living*, I thought, *for I had come to know a fate worse than death.* They pierced me with guilt trips and passive-aggressive taunts, torturing my headspace with things I knew to be true but refused to address.

A ping echoed from afar, signaling the arrival of a pod train. The doors opened and a throng of new moms joined the berating. I shoved my way towards the train, desperate to rid myself of gnawing truths. As the doors began to close, I surged forward with all my might and dove into the pod. I hit the floor and tumbled into the rear wall, knocking the wind from my lungs. When I turned back, the mother mass chided my career choice, then exploded into a cloud of fluttlenibs (read: helicopter butterflies with nagging dispositions). The pod pinged as if nothing was amiss, then proceeded to the next stop.

I spent the rest of the day inside that pod. I wanted to leave, but the doors had grown shark teeth and I didn't want to risk it.

Day Two

The fever continued inside the merchant district of a random ring. I did not leave the pod, so much as sail through the doors involuntarily. A large bloke had decided that the pod was his new lover and tossed me outside like a jealous suitor.

I wandered the district while trying to ignore the giant eyeball hovering over my head. Its bloodshot gaze and bright orange iris proved rather unsettling, but it never attacked. It seemed intensely fascinated by my actions, even going so far as to narrate my movements. I named it Blinky because it had no eyelids.

Day Three

I had actually gotten some sleep, thanks to a spooked clown and a swift punch to the face. When I awoke, I could hear a commotion in the distance. A crowd had gathered and sounded a bit unruly. Blinky insisted that we check it out, so we did. I poked my head into a loading bay to find a mob of pink skeletons fighting a nurkalu (read: giant hairy lobster on stilts). Apparently, that's all my brain needed to know. I grabbed a potted plant and joined the battle, which made total sense at the time.

Day Four

Three words: pantsless chandelier hunting.

Day Five

I now understood that Blinky was a magical faerie guarding a pot of gold. He denied it, of course, but my stubborn insistence convinced him otherwise. We boarded a pod train and ended up at an ocean ring beach. I spent the entire day digging holes in the sand based on cryptic clues. Blinky watched the effort with a voyeuristic hunger. As the pizza sun began to set, I passed out from exhaustion and fell into one of the holes.

Day Six

I awoke inside the hole, but Blinky was nowhere to be found. He had left a note that read, "There was no gold. I'm just a digging enthusiast." I shouted some gibberish and punched the sand five times, which summoned Veferaf, the Ocean Dragon. I scrambled out of the hole and met gazes with a towering water serpent hovering above the waves.

"Choose your cheese," the dragon said with a menacing growl. I removed my turquoise tie, wrapped it around my forehead, and struck a superhero pose. "Cheddar," I said, and fucking meant it. The dragon roared with displeasure and I shot a fireball at him. We fought into the evening.

Day Seven

I awoke feeling somewhat like myself, as did most of the population. I hadn't bathed in a week, so the ripeness of my body made its presence known. All that remained of my suit was a tattered jacket and a headband tie. I wandered the beach in a haze of confusion, as did several others. Eye contact was brief and uncomfortable. It took a while to pinpoint my location, but I eventually made it back to a pod station. When I arrived, a small group of citizens was waiting patiently for the next train. Some were bloody, some were naked, and nobody dared to comment on those facts. For the ultimate walk of shame had commenced.

* * *

In the end, the citizens of Durangoni had suffered an extraordinary loss, both economically and psychologically. Cleaning and rebuilding were equally painful, as shame was smeared across the station like a grisly crime scene. In order to cope, the population united under a shared layer of scar tissue. No one wanted to relive the time they awoke from a harrowing delusion, battered, bruised, and covered in mayonnaise.

Or hiding in a vat of engine grease with a missing finger.

Or perched atop a fountain while trying to impregnate it.

Or trapped inside an air duct while wearing assless chaps.

Or zealously stabbing every stuffed animal in a toy store.

Or stranded inside the Kink Rinks ... in any circumstance.

The Incident would remain exactly that, a generic event that everyone acknowledged, but refused to discuss. When the dust settled, I was tasked to record a brief yet conclusive entry for the directory. In its entirety: "A weeklong event where a trillion beings stared into the maw of madness, then went back to work."

Durangoni remains stubbornly tight-lipped about it. They only release footage for the most heinous of criminal investigations. The entire week is blacked out from the archives, and for good reason. By normal standards, most citizens would have faced prison time.

Security feeds leading up to The Incident are choppy at best. The most compelling comes from the Zandui Casino. A nameless citizen had won the Big Sixty jackpot, sparking a giant celebration before the feed crackled away. What should have been a station-wide news spectacle was quickly snuffed from existence.

The peculiar timing has spawned numerous conspiracy theories, from typical government mistrust to tinfoil hat lunacy. In the end, the only info revealed to the public was that Roy had won and no one could find him. His status as a sub-core plumber lit a fire of intrigue that would blossom into legend.

Praxie survived the ordeal, as she was observed several weeks later drinking heavily inside a Kink Rink pub. Roy, on the other hand, had disappeared entirely. The last known footage of his life aboard the station was captured at a remote banking outpost that serviced the needs of specialized traders. It flanked a seldom-used port and employed a small staff. Weeks after The Incident, Roy walked up to a teller window and withdrew 300 trillion credits onto a single mofu (mobile funding unit). He thanked the teller, who promptly fainted.

Roy exited the bank, turned a corner, and was never seen again.

CHAPTER 18

Years later, Durangoni had healed and moved past its collective woe. Conversations had returned to normal. Commerce had resumed its stride. Roy's status as a tenacious rebel had wormed its way into the public conscience. His name was toasted in bars, discussed in shops, and debated among the rich. After all, it's not every day that an unknown dreg can ensnare a trillion minds.

His legend was here to stay.

But alas, he remained a ghost.

I spent countless hours trying to uncover his tracks, but every lead brought me to another dead end. The story had gone cold, as did my excitement for piecing it together.

It was done.

The story of Roy had reached its logical yet disappointing conclusion.

But then, out of the cold reaches of nowhere, something snagged my attention. I wasn't looking for it. It just appeared, like a tasty mint on a comfy pillow. Before I could wrap this yarn and send it to the presses, I had one more person to visit.

* * *

The next morning, I found myself inside a familiar abode. The plants and aromas were oddly comforting, like visiting an old garden with lots of love and history. Duncan poured me a mug of tea and settled into his ratty chair. Same 'ol Duncan, same 'ol tea, but with a whole new level of implication.

Thank you for agreeing to meet with me on such short notice.

Sure thing, always up for a pleasurable chitchat. So what would you like to discuss?

As you know, I have been building the story of Roy with the hopeful aim of bringing it to a satisfying conclusion. But try as I might, I cannot progress past the banking outpost. For all intents and purposes, Roy simply disappeared.

(Duncan smiles and nods.)

I reached out to every possible lead I could think of. Former bosses, favorite hussies, the whole gamut. None of them have seen Roy or know of his whereabouts.

(Duncan smiles and nods again.)

I also consulted financial records, hoping to uncover large transactions from mysterious sources of wealth. Again, nothing.

(Duncan smiles and nods again.)

However, in doing so, my updated records showed a peculiar abnormality. I was hoping that you could shed some light on it.

Oh boy, you got me on the pins and needles.

With your permission, I would like you to verify some statements.

Permission granted. Toss me some teasers.

Hours before Roy won the Big Sixty jackpot, security footage shows him making a hasty phone call. It is rumored that the

game's unbeatable algorithm wasn't an algorithm at all. It was a pure randomization governed by the big red button located in the entry corridor of The Pipes community pub. An area that, all too conveniently, has no security feed.

Is that right? Well isn't that a hoot. I've pressed Big Red many times myself.

Shortly before the winning block started, the sole security feed inside The Pipes shows you leaving the bar. You returned after the block ended and ordered another drink.

Yes sir.

(I let the statement linger, then shrug.)

Oh, you think they're connected in some fashion.

Seems like a reasonable conclusion.

Well I'm sorry to disappoint, but I think you found yourself a coinkydink. You see, my bowel movements are something of a multi-flush affair, if you catch my drift. (He pats his pudgy belly and laughs.)

You take hour-long shits?

Yes sir. Sometimes longer, if I've had some shellfish. Worth it, though.

Duncan, you work for a mid-tier construction company.

Yes.

And you live in the sub-core.

Yes.

The average bank balance for a sub-core resident is around 2,000 credits.

Seems reasonable, yes.

And yet, your account shows an active balance of 299 *trillion* credits.

Yes sir.

(The matter-of-fact response gives me pause. A brief silence grips the room.)

And that doesn't strike you as odd?

It's more than the average Joseph, that's for sure.

More than the—Duncan, you can purchase an entire ring on the Durangoni Space Station for that amount of cash.

Yes sir.

(I glance around his humble abode and quickly regain eye contact, asking the next question without asking the question.)

(chuckles) Not much interest in the fancy floof. I like my job, I like my place, and I enjoy being part of this community. And besides, moving is such a fuss.

Duncan, you could arrange to have the entire community physically detached from the station and relocated to its own moon.

I suppose. But something else would need to fill the void, y'know? I feel like I'm where I need to be. I can't help the lowlies if I gots a moon to govern. I can do more down here than I could ever do up there.

(An understanding settles between us. We both knew what had happened, and we recognized the merits of the outcome. Duncan was, and continued to be, the most genuine and dignified person I have ever had the pleasure of meeting. He deserved every cent, and would use his fortune to better the world around him. Roy knew that. And yet, there I was, a lowly reporter with a valueless job to do. He knew the question was coming, and I knew it would be inconsequential. But we both understood that it needed to be asked.)

Do you know where Roy is?

No sir.

Would you tell me if you did?

Oh yes. I would love nothing more than to place a big shiny bow atop this tale of intrigue.

Any idea of where he could be?

No sir.

Do you think he would ever come back here?

One can only hope. We would all love to see Roy again. In fact, I paid the rent on his unit for the next 500 years.

(I flinch in response.) *What?* Why?

Roy is a hero to the sub-core folk. He's a symbol of hope and determination, of what can be if you keep waking up. It seemed only right that his unit be maintained as a shrine to his legacy. The door is always unlocked if you fancy a gander. Workers from far and wide venture down here every day to pay their respects.

That's ... that's actually kind of beautiful.

Seems like a fitting end to the story, doncha think?

(Of course it didn't, but I knew what he meant. Duncan would not provide the closure that I richly desired. But oddly enough, the visit did feel conclusive. I nod, smile, and stand from my chair.)

I do. And I thank you for the kindness.

You betcha.

(We exchange a final pleasantry and I begin the long trek back to my own world. I pass Roy's unit in the hallway, but decide

not to visit. I knew it would yield nothing useful, as did Duncan.)

* * *

And thus concludes the story of Roy, the incredible tale of a zero to hero who united us all through a psychotropic mind-fuck. His enduring impact lives inside our collective conscience. We all remember where we were when The Incident ravaged Durangoni. We also remember where we ended up, for better or for worse. It tore us apart to bring us together, and in a very perverse way, we owe Roy a debt of gratitude.

He was an agent of chaos that we bested as one.

Roy is gone, but not forgotten. Adored, yet misunderstood. His tale continues somewhere in the cosmos. We wish him well, curse his existence, and hope to see him soon.

THE END

Find more tales of intrigue at:
PukiHorpocket.com

Zachry Wheeler is an award-winning science fiction novelist, screen-writer, and coffee slayer. He enjoys English football, stand-up comedy, and is known to lurk around museums and brewpubs. His series works include the Immortal Wake, Max and the Multiverse, and Puki Horpocket Presents.

Learn more at **ZachryWheeler.com**

If you enjoyed this nutty tale, please consider posting a short review on Amazon. Ratings and reviews are the currency by which authors gain visibility. They are the single greatest way to show your support and keep us writing the stories that you love.

Thank you for reading!

Manufactured by Amazon.ca
Acheson, AB